operation prom date

Tactics in Flirting Series

operation prom date

Tactics in Flirting Series

CINDI MADSEN

Entangled Publishing, LLC
2614 South Timberline Road
Suite 109
Fort Collins, CO 80525
Visit our website at www.entangledpublishing.com.

Crush is an imprint of Entangled Publishing, LLC.

Edited by Stacy Abrams and Alexa May
Cover design by Erin Dameron-Hill
Cover art from iStock

Manufactured in the United States of America

First Edition March 2017

To Kylie, my favorite person for discussions about shipping couples, canons, OTPs, & every other term that completely baffles your dad because he has absolutely no clue what we're talking about. I'm so lucky that I get to be your mom.

Chapter One

KATE

Sometimes in life you had to make the best of a crappy situation. Like how instead of sulking over my lack of vehicular transport and the fact that my mom was running late—*again*—I used it as an excuse to sit in the parking lot near the football field, drinking a soda, working on my tan, and watching the boys scrimmage (i.e., watching the way their muscles flexed as they threw, ran, caught, and tackled one another).

Which was especially intriguing, since one set of muscles belonged to Mick, the guy I'd had a crush on for the past year. Okay, maybe more like the last two years if I were being totally honest, but there were periods in there when I'd *tried* to abandon it for guys who were more in my league.

Unfortunately, it never worked. For one, I was flirtationally challenged, but two, I still compared them all to the guy with the dark messy hair, soulful blue eyes, and did I mention the muscles? He was the quarterback of our team, and he liked to keep in shape between seasons—he had offers from several different universities to play next year, from our local New Hampshire University to one down in Florida and all the way to one on the west coast. Lucky university, whichever one snagged him.

To say I had it bad for him…? Well, that was a huge freaking understatement. The middle of sophomore year, when everyone else tromped over my dropped notebook as I struggled to balance my armload of textbooks, he'd stopped. After shaking his head at the rude passersby—he even muttered a "really, dudes?"—he picked up my slightly beat-up notebook, wiped off the dirt, and handed it over with a grin.

A zing of electricity traveled up my arm, cartoon birds chirped overhead, and in that moment, I saw the sweet guy under the cool jock exterior.

My crush only grew the day he came into the ice cream shop after school with his little brother. I was there doing my homework, waiting for Mom as usual. He nodded at me, one corner of his lips kicking up, and more than my ice cream melted.

Since then I'd thought up a dozen scenarios where we exchanged more than pleasantries, he realized I was awesome, and we held hands and kissed and basically made everyone jealous of how cute we were.

Now that we were well into our last semester of senior year, with college on the horizon, I'd decided *this* was the semester I was going to make him mine. Whatever it took.

A tall shadow cut off my sunshine, which made my legs look tanner but would prevent them from actually tanning if whoever it was didn't move. I glanced up. And up, and up. Cooper Callihan grew taller every year, and he had to be past six feet now. He'd also filled out this year, which looked good on him, but meant he blocked more of my sun.

A crooked grin curved his mouth. "Still interested in Pecker, I see."

"*Shhh!*" I glared at him, trying to convey that I'd ruin his life if anyone overheard. He didn't seem scared. I also hated that he called Mick by his surname. Yes, it was a rather unfortunate last name, and from what I could tell, Mick's only flaw. Of course when you looked like he did, you made it work for you anyway.

I glanced at Mick—still a good twenty or so yards away, thank goodness—then back at Cooper. We were sort of friends, as in we shared a history class where we'd been partnered together for a project and had hung out during one summer at the lake a few years ago, when he was just a scrawny guy who spouted a lot of facts about the stars. I'd once been his rowing partner during a trip across the lake, but that was mostly by default, since my former BF *not* F convinced me to go with him so she could be alone with Donovan Lawson.

I twirled the end of my ponytail around my finger, noticing the tips of my brown hair were lightening thanks to the past few weeks of sunshine. "So you…you can tell? That I…?" I couldn't say it aloud for fear someone else would hear, even as I looked around to confirm we were alone. I lowered my voice to a whisper. "Do you think *he's* noticed?"

Cooper moved to sit on the parking curb next to me, bumping his hip into mine when there wasn't enough room—the guy had boundary issues, obviously. I scooted over, though, anxious to hear his answer.

"He's probably noticed," he said, leaning back on his palms and tipping his face to the sun. Of course he was still blocking half my access.

My cheeks heated and I groaned, fighting the urge to look over at Mick again. Then I sighed, my entire body deflating. "That means he would've done something about it if he were actually interested."

"Not necessarily."

I waited for more, but Cooper just sat there, the sun lighting up his mop of dirty blond, slightly out-of-control wavy hair. "Explain."

"I…" He shot me a sidelong glance and shook his head. "I'm not sure that's a good idea." The urge to storm away was strong, but that wouldn't help with my goal to win over Mick this semester. If I worked fast enough, maybe we could even go to prom together—after all, I'd been talked into being on the decorating committee, and it'd be so sad to decorate but not attend. The image of the two of us entering a decorated gym, me in a sparkly dress and Mick sporting a dapper tux and his trademark sexy smirk hit me, and longing rose up.

Wait. Do people say dapper *anymore?* Well, it was my imaginary dream prom. He could look dapper, and the more I thought about it, the stronger the longing grew.

That's it. No more being passive and waiting for it to magically happen. I'm going to make *it happen.* And I had just about two months to do it, which meant I needed to get started ASAP.

Since I was already swimming in maximum embarrassment level, I decided to dive right in and see how big of a challenge I was in for.

"Spill now," I said. "Or leave my perch."

Cooper arched an eyebrow. Just as I was about to give him a shove and reclaim my curb, he gave a resigned sigh and said, "It might not be that he's completely uninterested. You're a pretty girl and all. You just…come across as a chick who wants a serious thing."

I frowned. "That's probably because I do."

"I know. And it shows."

My lungs tightened, refusing to take in or expel oxygen. "So glad we established that. I think I'll go now. See if I can't find some poison ivy to roll around in to top off this delightful afternoon."

As I started to stand, Cooper caught my arm. "I'm not trying to insult you."

"Then what are you trying to do?"

He shrugged. "Help."

"So far, you're doing a bang-up job."

He grinned, because apparently he didn't understand English. "Hey, you're the one who insisted on an explanation." I'd forgotten how frustrating he could be with his blasé attitude—it drove me crazy when I was trying to ensure we got an A on our history project. No wonder we'd never become closer friends. "How many girls have you seen Pecker with through the years?"

"His name is Mick."

"What kind of name is that, anyway?" Cooper took a large swig of *my* soda. "It's like his parents got halfway through naming him and just stopped in the middle."

"His parents met at a Rolling Stones concert—he's named after one of the greatest rock stars of all times, which I think is pretty cool."

"'Cool' isn't the word I'd use. And you know way too much about him. Now, answer the question."

I had to think past the ridiculous name discussion to remember his question. "He averages three girls a semester." When Cooper's forehead crinkled, I clarified. "Two the first half of junior year, three the second, and four last semester."

"So you're a math girl."

"I…dabble." *If by dabble, you mean I can differentiate and integrate in my sleep.*

I was a bit of a math nerd, but I tried to keep it on the down low. I was actually pretty proud Cooper didn't know that about me already. Although, like Oliver Queen on *Arrow*, people found out my secret at an alarming rate. Pretty soon all of Starling City—er, Auburn—would know.

Maybe I've been hitting Netflix a little too hard as of late. As if I didn't already struggle enough keeping in touch with reality.

"Okay, so what about those girls' averages?" Cooper asked, enough of a grin on his face that his already conspicuous dimples stood out even more.

"You mean average intelligence?"

Cooper laughed, and despite my earlier annoyance, I found I was now semi-glad he'd stopped to harass me. "I meant more what do they have in common," he said. "How serious do they come across?"

"Not very, since they also have several guys they hook up with during the course of the school year." I already had bad blood with Paris Townsend, one of Mick's on-and-off again girls, which probably made me more judgmental than I should be. "They just go from boy to boy like it's nothing."

"Exactly."

I could feel my eyebrows scrunching together but couldn't help it. "But if I get another boyfriend, I won't have time to actually land Mick. Especially at the rate I go."

"He just needs to see you as a non-serious or high-maintenance type. Once you catch his interest, you play it cool, and if you do it right, *he'll* be the one chasing *you.*"

"Okay. Yeah. I can do that." I gave one sharp nod, because it seemed like the move to make when you got serious about something, and I was now super-duper serious about Operation Land Mick As My Prom Date.

That's kind of long. Maybe I should just cut it down to Operation Prom Date.

"Good luck." With that, Cooper tossed my now-empty Dr Pepper can in the recycling bin—so at least he recycled, and I supposed that helped negate the fact that he'd finished off my soda—and started away from me.

Panic immediately set in.

I didn't know how to catch Mick's interest or play it cool. Overthinking was my middle name. Not to mention I only had a couple of months—less, really, because people usually had dates at least a month in advance—and with the margin for error I required, that wasn't nearly enough time.

"Wait," I said, and Cooper slowly turned around. I jumped to my feet and moved over to him, wanting to make sure no one else heard this conversation. Embarrassing as it was, I was in over my head. My past failures to have more than five-minute conversations with Mick proved that. Cooper's male perspective made me realize I needed to go about things in a different way, and I needed more of that insight. "I don't know how to snag his interest or play it cool. I…need help."

I couldn't believe what I was about to say, but Cooper had gone from the scrawny dude who talked astronomy nonstop to a rowing star who fit in with any and every group. Unlike me, he had the whole popular thing down. He already knew about my crush, too, so at this point, I figured I didn't have much to lose. "Could you maybe show me how? Please?"

Chapter Two

How did I land myself in this mess? All I'd wanted was an afternoon on the water. Instead, I found out that my rowing partner jacked up his wrist and was going to be out for at least three weeks, maybe four.

As I cut across the field to get to my truck, I spotted Kate and thought I'd ask if she needed a ride—she lived just outside of the district and I knew that her mom often worked crazy hours. When I noticed her longingly looking at Pecker—the same look I'd witnessed a couple of months ago when we were working on our history project in the library and he'd walked in—I couldn't help but comment. Half the girls in school went crazy over the guy, who, in my opinion, was kind of a jerk.

Okay, I might be biased, since my major beef with the guy started last year at the Spring Festival, after his team beat mine in the annual race across the lake. Sure, it was in two-man wooden rowboats, not boats specifically designed to glide through the water as quickly as possible, but rowing was my thing. I'd competed with my eight-man team at State and won, after all. How could Mr. Preppy Football Player beat me?

The answer was he had a better partner. This year, I made sure that I'd have the better one—and I had, until the idiot got drunk over the weekend, fell out of a tree, and tore a ligament in his damn wrist. *He'd better be ready to go by the festival, or I'll…*

Even mentally threatening to re-injure his wrist seemed too harsh, tempting or not. More than anything, I was just grouchy that I might not get as much time on the lake as he healed. It was easier to convince my parents to let all those hours slide when it involved someone else.

I'd called everyone in my list of rowing contacts, only to find people were already paired up to train for that race or other events, or busy with another sport—baseball, lacrosse, track. *Dang overachievers.*

"Cooper, are you even listening to me?" Kate waved her arms and stuck her full bottom lip out in a pout. "I'm practically begging here, and my pride is already injured. The least you could do is answer me."

I pulled my full attention back to Kate. Like I said, it wasn't that she wasn't pretty—with her big green eyes, long dark hair, and laidback jeans-and-T-shirt style, she had the wholesome girl next door look. But she always came across as a girl who was serious about life in general—I knew firsthand how seriously she took her class assignments and grades—and the type of girl who'd definitely demand exclusivity. Mick Pecker would never go for that, not unless she was someone else's girl and he wanted to take her away for sport.

"What do you need?" she asked, sticking a fist on her hip. "Help in a math class? I'm also pretty good at science. Or I can…knit sweaters or scarfs or beanies."

"You knit? Wow. That's…something my grandma does."

She made an exasperated noise, somewhere between a growl and a sigh. "You know what? Never mind. I don't want your stupid help." She grabbed her backpack and started away, throwing the words "You probably couldn't even pull it off anyway" over her shoulder.

The side of me that loved a challenge perked up. My main goals for the rest of this semester were sliding through my classes and lots of time in my boat, but I could use a little more adventure, especially since once this summer ended and college started, my life was basically over. It'd be a degree in something mundane like political science or criminal justice, then three years of law school, then sitting in an office and practicing boring law, because that's what Callihan men did.

I quickened my steps to catch up with her. "Hold on."

She spun around and narrowed her eyes. Yikes. The girl could give a serious dirty look, even though her sweet features still didn't quite match her deadly expression. "You owe me, you know. Who gave the bulk of our presentation on World War One when you were"—she made air quotes—"*so tired* from your last rowing competition?"

I'd been so slammed last semester, and she'd taken point, no complaints. "You got me there. I would've never scored that A without you." Which gave me an idea…I'd seen how focused and determined she got. How organized she was. That attention to detail and time management was exactly what I needed to up my training right now. Plus, I remembered how she'd surprised me with how well she handled a boat on the lake a few summers ago. "I have a proposition for you…"

Her eyes narrowed further, suspicion mixing in.

"My rowing partner for the Spring Festival race busted his wrist, and I need to keep up my training. How about you be my partner until he recovers?"

She wrinkled her nose.

"You asked what I needed. Not only do I need to keep up my training to ensure a top spot on Harvard's rowing team, I want to win the Spring Festival race, and I've seen you out on the lake, remember? You can handle yourself in a boat. Plus, Pec—Mick—always enters that race, too, and he's out on the water practicing sometimes. It'll only help land his attention."

Her posture relaxed a fraction. "I'm listening…"

Was I really doing this? Hell, if anything, the girl was highly entertaining, and if it came down to me alone on the boat trying to keep track of everything while juggling the oars, or having Kate along to keep me on task and provide a more accurate picture of a two-person race, that seemed like the better option. Added bonus, it provided the time-commitment-to-someone excuse that would help keep Dad off my back. "Train with me, and I'll train you on how to land Mick."

She shushed me again. "Seriously, you always say it so loud. I don't think you can be discreet, and if this got out…" She hugged her arms around her middle as if she needed to protect herself.

"It won't. I'll be more discreet. I'll help you, and I guarantee that by the end of the month"—I lowered my voice—"Mick will be the one staring at *you*."

She seemed to be mentally weighing her options. "How long do I have to train with you?"

"Until Jaden's wrist heals. Probably three weeks, maybe four." If it took a whole month, that'd only give Jaden and me one week of practice until the actual race, but at least I'd stay strong enough to make up for it.

"Three or four weeks? That's intense." She pressed her lips together, resolve settling into her features, and then her gaze lifted to mine. "I want him to do more than stare. I want him to go to prom with me."

Prom? Shit, when this girl went for it, she really went for it.

Most girls were obsessed with that one special night dancing among cheesy decorations, while most guys couldn't care less, except that it meant their dates might be more adventurous.

Kate's face dropped, and I got the feeling I'd accidentally insulted her by not responding with a resounding yes to being able to make it happen. "Easy peasy," I said, then considered kicking my own ass.

"Easy peasy?" she asked with a giggle.

Great. The girl who liked to knit and solve equations was mocking me. Good thing I didn't care what anyone at this school thought about me. "Just don't tell me you're planning on knitting your dress."

She shoved me. "I'm already regretting admitting anything to you. But fine. Your deal is acceptable." She held out her hand, apparently wanting to shake on it—I'd remark that it was the kind of gesture that gave off the serious vibe, but decided I better hold off until we'd sealed the deal.

I shook her hand. Her skin was crazy soft, her hand so small compared to mine, and I couldn't help but notice the bright blue nails.

The zing that raced through my veins surprised me, but like I said, I did love a challenge. Not that I'd admit to how big of a one it was to her, but I had a feeling she'd have a lot of competition.

A smile curved her lips. "Operation Prom Date is go for launch."

"You named it?"

"What? I'm supposed to wait for you to come up with a clever name? Likely story."

I bit back a laugh—she was a little more bonkers than I realized. *Yep, these next few weeks will definitely be amusing, if nothing else.*

An older SUV pulled into the parking lot, and Kate released my hand and hiked her bag higher on her shoulder.

"Meet me tomorrow after school for training," I said. "I'll give you a ride home after, but fair warning, you'll get back sort of late."

"That's okay. I usually do my homework in class anyway."

As she walked away, I noticed the way her long ponytail swayed in time with her hips. So the girl might be on the serious side, but I could definitely work with that.

Chapter Three

What did one wear for her first day of being Play it Cool Kate, with a side of rowing training? After all, seduction and sports hardly went together.

Unless you happened to be Mick, then throwing a ball was alluring enough. Come to think of it, most any guy seemed sexier while playing sports, making me rethink my stance on seduction and sports.

It didn't seem to work the same for women, though, which was totally unfair. Or maybe I just had no clue what guys found sexy. According to Cooper, it was mostly not being serious. If anyone had the not-serious market pegged, it was the guy who strolled through the halls of the school like he didn't have a care in the world. I pulled my flamingo shirt out of my drawer. The words "majestically awkward" curved above the bird that had one leg up in the air and was about to fall. Mom and I saw it in a store and we'd both laughed at how accurately it described me.

"I highly doubt that's the type of not-seriousness guys are looking for." Which was why I mostly wore it during Netflix binges on the weekend.

Mom's head popped through the open door. "What did you say, hon?"

"Nothing. Just talking to myself." *Like a normal person.*

I glanced at the glass cage where Klaus, my bearded dragon, slept, thinking I should've at least claimed I was talking to him. He peeked an eye open as I patted his head and then settled back down for another long day of napping. Clearly he cared a lot about what I wore.

"Okay, well hurry up. We've got to be out the door in fifteen." She rushed down the hall toward her bedroom.

I crossed to my shelves, where my jewelry box sat among my Funko Pop collection, and put on my three-tiered gold necklace. Naturally, I'd paired up the figurines in the couplings they should be in, whether or not the TV show or book series they belonged to was currently doing the right thing and allowing them to be together.

You'd think all my time spent analyzing fictional relationships would help me have one of my own. But those relationships probably only gave me false expectations, because outside of movies, books, and TV, the most popular guy in school didn't usually notice the smart, semi-awkward girl who would be perfect for him.

But Cooper's going to help me, and it'll all work out. I still couldn't believe the deal I'd struck with him. Two summers ago he was just the scrawny guy Amber and I constantly bumped into as we were running around by Massabesic Lake. They both lived nice and close to the banks, the sparkling water visible from their big front windows. That was back in the day when she and I were best friends, before I learned what betrayal felt like. It was also back when Cooper talked about constellations a lot. He knew them all, and one night he pointed out several with this app he had on his phone.

Amber had told him no one cared, so to stop rattling off boring facts, and while I didn't agree, I didn't stand up for him, either. I usually just went along with whatever she said. It was how being her friend worked. It made me feel stupid now, but back then I'd been the new girl who'd transferred because her mom thought her other school's students were too rough, their classes too basic. The basic classes theory was true, the too rough debatable. Auburn Academy was also closer to the real estate office where she worked and showed houses, and as a parent now doing the job of two, that made a huge difference for both of us.

Honestly, I liked it at AA better, although my status as the kid on the far outskirts, the lake nowhere in viewing range, sometimes made me feel like an outsider. Not that I didn't appreciate our charming—if a bit outdated—two-bedroom house that boasted a view of lots and lots of trees. Unless Mr. Morris was working on his vehicles or RV in his yard, when our view had a bit more butt crack than I preferred.

I crossed the hall to Mom's room and opened her summer drawer. A tangerine beaded tank top sat on top, and I decided it was just what I was looking for. And that my mom was cooler than me, but I tried not to linger on that thought.

Apparently I took more after my dad when it came to style—we went for easy and comfy. After all, we never knew when one of our impromptu "top-secret missions" would crop up.

My gaze automatically lifted to the picture of my parents on top of the dresser. The sorrow that pressed against my chest was a ghost of what it used to be, something that faded a bit more every year, although I knew it'd always be with me. He'd enlisted in the Air Force in order to help pay for an engineering degree, but then he fell in love with flying.

Constant deployments were all I'd ever known, those

long stretches without my dad. They passed by slowly, but Mom and I would gradually adjust and get used to it being just us. Then he'd be home for about a year.

But last deployment we lost him for good, and there was a big difference between missing him because he wasn't home for long stretches and missing him because he was never coming home. That was two and a half years ago—sometimes it felt like an eternity and sometimes it felt like yesterday. It just depended on the day.

"Kate! I swear if you don't get your butt in the car in five minutes, I'm going to leave you!"

An empty threat, but I hustled all the same, quickly exchanging my T-shirt for the flashy tank top. I resisted the urge to throw my hair in a ponytail and stopped in my room for lip-gloss and my backpack before taking the stairs two at a time and rushing out the door.

By the time I arrived in the passenger seat, I was out of breath.

Mom looked at me, her eyebrows scrunching together.

"What?" I smoothed a hand down the shirt. "Does this not look okay?"

"I like it. I'm just wondering what inspired the change in fashion."

"Just felt like trying something new." Like trying to actually land my crush instead of staring at him from afar. Usually I told Mom quite a bit about school and my crushes, but I knew she would tell me to just be myself, and it was hard to convince her that being myself simply wasn't cutting it. She didn't understand, because she was the kind of woman who got attention from attractive men all the time. She accidentally flirted, as in it took no effort or thought and she didn't even realize she was coming across as flirty.

Whereas even the thought of talking to my crush made my palms start to sweat.

So for right now, Operation Prom Date would remain on a classified, need-to-know basis. And I was as surprised as anyone that it somehow included Cooper Callihan.

Chapter Four

KATE

If I thought something as simple as a change in wardrobe, wearing my hair down, and putting on a necklace and an extra coat of shimmery lip-gloss would produce head-turning results—and I kind of hoped it'd be that easy—I would be wrong.

I mean, the guy with the locker next to mine at least gave me a smile before asking me to please move aside. Considering the aroma coming off his clothing, I think it had more to do with herbal help than an appreciation of my going out on a fashion limb.

My former BFF Amber didn't seem to notice as she, Paris, and their clique rushed past me, not a single glance spared in my direction. More than anything, I felt invisible, which was pretty much how I felt every day.

Sometimes I wondered if I could go back in time and do things differently, if I would. Amber said she wanted to start hanging out with Paris and her group, so I'd tried. But Paris made Amber's pushiness look mild, and when I wasn't cool with her talking down to me and trying to make me a minion, I didn't stick around.

When I relayed how I felt to Amber over the phone, she told me she understood, and since they were semi-horrible to her, too, we agreed to break off on our own again. Only the next week at school, she pretended I didn't exist and stuck with Paris and her crew, making it clear she'd picked them and the promise of popularity over me. It hurt, and it didn't help that without her to hang out with, my mind had more time to dwell on how much I missed my dad and how empty my house was with Mom working all the time. But it was about a year ago, so I was mostly over it. I wasn't sure if I missed who she used to be more, or if I just missed having a close friend.

No use crying over spilled friendships. Especially not today.

Last night I'd thought about it, and in addition to putting a little more effort into my clothing—but not so much effort I came across as too serious or high-maintenance—I was going to talk to Mick. Even if it was a simple hi. I had to start somewhere, right?

I spotted Cooper's head above the crowd, his blond waves messy as usual, and thought about going to ask him about my wardrobe choice and for help with possible conversation topics. After all, it'd be awesome if my "hi" to Mick turned into more. But he was laughing with a group of people, a junior girl on the fringe hanging on his every word, and the risk of someone overhearing was way too high. No reason to turn my already difficult mission into a suicide mission.

Besides, my first class of the day was in the other direction, and I couldn't be late. Just the thought made my heart pick up its pace.

Hugging my books to my chest, I wove my way down the hall.

Mick was coming up, a couple of his boys around him.

Okay, this is it. Give him a flirty smile.

Say hi.

I licked my lips, my courage floundering. The non-flavored lip-gloss didn't help, either. Sparkly was cool and all, but could they not make it taste like…well, grossness?

Then again, there was that time back in elementary school when I ate an entire stick of banana Lip Smacker. I got super sick and couldn't stand artificial banana flavor to this day.

O-M-G, focus, Kate! He's almost past you! Just do something…

I cleared my throat. Yeah, apparently my knee-jerk reaction is to make a sound like an old person clearing phlegm. Ugh, seriously, why were all my internal thoughts dwelling on disgusting things today?

For the briefest moment, Mick's gaze flickered my way. I started to lift my hand in a wave, but then my books slipped, and I had to concentrate on keeping them from falling. Yes, our only conversation involved him picking up my dropped notebook, but if I went around doing that all the time he'd only think I was a klutz, and that was hardly the impression I wanted to make on him.

Still, the movement must've caught his eye, and I swear his attention lingered. On me!

I opened my mouth, because this was my chance to cross talking to him off my list. A strand of hair fell in my face and stuck to that extra coat of lip-gloss I'd slicked on. I quickly swiped at it, trying to pull it off as more of a sexy hair-flip, and went for try two of making words.

"Hey, Kate!" Isaiah, one of the guys in my AP Calculus class, approached. "Did you do the bonus problems for calc? I wanted to see if we got the same answer."

Oliver Queen, I totally understand the struggle now. Secret identities are really hard to keep up. Okay, so mine might be slightly less detrimental to my continuing to be alive and stuff, but with Mick now headed away from me, all the air in my lungs stuck in there, making it hard to breathe.

I'd never ignore someone who'd been a real friend to me, though, so I shot Isaiah the smile I'd been preparing for Mick. "Yeah, I did them all. What did you get?"

As he pulled out his homework, I tried to tell myself that some problems took more work to get right.

I'd try again.

But my brain hated me, because a countdown flashed through it, and I wondered how I'd ever land Mick as my prom date when I couldn't even manage a simple hello.

Chapter Five

I leaned against the sun-warmed hood of my truck after school as I waited for Kate. I checked the time on my phone again. What was taking her so long? I wanted to get out on the lake so badly I'd practically sprinted through the double doors.

Finally I spotted her trailing out with the other people who were clearly not in a hurry to leave the place, mostly thanks to the orange shirt that stood out in the crowd. I waved and she started over to me. The sun glinted off her necklace and she squinted at me, putting a hand over her eyes to shield them.

"Operation Prom Date did not go so well today," she said with a sigh.

"You asked him to prom?" I'd thought we were going to build up to that.

"No! Do you think I'm crazy?"

"You probably don't want me to answer that."

She smacked me. She seemed to do that a lot, especially considering we were two for two in as many days.

I opened the door for her, partly because I liked to think I could be a gentleman sometimes, but mostly because I was in a hurry and wanted her to get her butt in my truck so we could leave already.

As soon as she was seated, I rushed around the front, climbed in, and fired up the engine. I glanced over at Kate as I turned out of the parking lot and headed toward Massabesic Lake. "Sometimes Jaden and I drive into Manchester and practice with the Central Crew Club on the Merrimack River, but I think it'll be better to start you in the lake."

"Isn't that where the Spring Festival race is going to be anyway?"

"Yeah, but if I practice against the current in the river, I'll kill it on the lake—or say it's windy, it won't be a big deal."

"Where does Mick practice?"

"It depends on the day. It's not like I ask him."

"Well, how am I supposed to get his attention if he's at the river and I'm at the lake, or vice versa?"

Of course I hadn't given a second thought to where Pecker might be training today, or if he even was. I hoped he wasn't, and that he was wasting time playing football instead. Then again, it'd be more satisfying to beat him if he'd given his all. "Trust me, we're going to get him to notice you. The training is only one part of my plan."

She spun to face me, the green scenery blurring in the window behind her. "Oh, good, so you actually have a plan. I was starting to think you just needed a boating partner and I was a sucker."

I froze, then did my best to smother any trace of guilt that might've crossed my features when she hit a little too close to the truth. I didn't have a solid plan for her crazy scheme—or operation, as she'd chosen to call it. That'd require giving thought to it. I'd been far too focused on my relief over finding a temporary fill-in to train with. But I didn't think Kate was a sucker. Now, thinking she had shitty taste in guys, on the other hand...

Realizing that her arched eyebrows must mean she wanted me to explain my grand plan, I turned down the radio as if I were about to say something super profound. "Remember how you're supposed to be playing it cool? Stop stressing. Just leave the planning to me."

There. That should buy me at least a night to come up with something.

"Playing it cool and being clueless are two different things," she said. "In order to even relax enough to fake the blasé attitude that comes so naturally to you, I need to know there's a plan."

"Blasé attitude? That's how you think about me?"

"Yeah. You're like Mr. Cool, nothing gets to you."

I wished I felt that way. I supposed at school all I cared about was getting good enough grades that my parents wouldn't call me in for a meeting. School was easy enough. Home was where I walked on pins and needles.

"I've actually envied it a bit before," Kate continued. "I remember two summers ago, when you were usually off by yourself in your boat, and it didn't seem to bother you in the least. And that night when everyone told you they didn't care about constellations so to stop pointing them out, you just shrugged it off and kept on stargazing."

"Well, *you* were nice about it." Honestly, it'd stung a little—how was I supposed to know not everyone found the universe over our heads fascinating? But Kate humored me for a few minutes, doing her best to act interested. "You even let me show you the constellation app I'd just downloaded."

"I thought it was kind of cool. But I couldn't say as much, because back then I had all that street cred."

I laughed. "Sorry I almost screwed that up."

"Clearly I didn't hold on to it for very long. I think it was just the new girl allure. It wore off quickly."

"I haven't thought about that summer in a while." All those nights when we were too young to drive anywhere and college was forever away, so we just ran around the lake, getting into what trouble we could with whoever we ran into. At the time, it was mostly Donovan and Amber, because they lived on either side of me. And Kate, because she was always at Amber's. "You and Amber were connected at the hip back then."

A flash of hurt crossed her features. "Things change." She picked at a thread on her jeans. "In the end, I wasn't cool enough for Amber—and apparently, I'm also too serious—and you got all tall and ripped and moved up to Mr. Cool and Confident."

I turned down the road that'd take us to the dock nearest my house.

"I want to focus on how you said I'm ripped…"

She shot me a look.

"*But* I'm going to point out that I didn't say you're too serious. All I said was that your more serious nature was probably why Pecker hasn't asked you out."

"It's not like he'd have any competition, though. Which brings me back to me." She dropped her head in her hands. "Maybe this whole thing is stupid and I should just give up now."

"Hey, no giving up." I parked and looked across the cab of my truck at her, trying to find the right pep talk to give. I just didn't have much experience in anything remotely close to this. In rowing, there were lots of cheesy sayings like "when you feel like you can no longer row with your arms, row with your heart" or "medals last longer than pain."

None of those would work, so I went for the truth. "Most

of the people we go to school with are idiots who need to be knocked over the head in order to pay attention to anything besides themselves. Me included."

She glanced up, part of her hair still covering her face in a way that framed her eyes and lips.

Most of the girls at school had that cookie cutter type look, a lot of them pretty, but so similar they blended together. Kate stood out. Honestly, why *weren't* guys asking her out? I'd considered it a few years ago, during that summer we'd spent time together. If I thought she was even a little interested, I might've. The night under the stars when she'd let me show her my constellation app, pity was the main vibe I got. Even when we'd ended up in my boat together by default, her attention was on Amber and Donovan in the other boat, and when I suggested veering in a different direction and leaving them behind for a while, she said we'd better not.

Now I knew her taste in guys ran toward the preppy super jock side, I knew I wasn't even close to her type.

Oops. Got a bit distracted during my big speech. "But not to fear. You've got me on your side now, and idiots or not, we'll snag their attention. Once we get even a few guys to take notice, the rest will follow, and then Mick will be as good as yours."

A smile slowly worked its way across her lips, lighting up the rest of her features along the way. "You really think so?"

I nodded. "By the way, I like that shirt. The bright color suits you." I'd like to think that was the least macho thing I'd ever said, but I did used to point out constellations and the mythology behind them, and then go into how stars were actually formed. Not to mention the inordinate amount of talking I used to do about Saturn's beautiful rings that were composed of ice particles, rocky debris, and dust.

"Thanks," she said, making me feel less self-conscious about doling out fashion compliments. "I figured if I'm going to do this, I might as well give it my all."

I glanced out at the glassy water and the antsy feeling over getting out there rose to the surface again. "I hope you plan on putting that same dedication into our rowing sessions."

She saluted me. "Aye, aye, Captain."

I chuckled as I climbed out of the truck. After gathering the gear, I moved over to untie the boat. "If you think I look ripped, just wait till you see what I can do with these muscles." Flashing her an over-the-top grin, I flexed like I was in one of those muscle-man competitions where they wore unspeakably small banana hammocks.

She shook her head as she fought back a smile. "Oh my gosh, that's like an eight on the Kanye Douchebag Scale."

Instead of arguing, I slid on my sunglasses and gave her a *what-up* nod. She lost the battle she'd been warring with her mouth and a killer smile broke free, filling me with a sense of accomplishment. Even though Kate was the type of girl who smiled often, I liked to think I got a bigger one than most. The way it lit up her entire face made me start calculating ways to keep it there permanently.

As I helped her into the boat, I vowed to give this whole operation thing more thought. Because Kate was a good person, and if she wanted to go to prom with a self-involved prick, I'd make sure it happened.

Chapter Six

KATE

My shoulders and arms ached, and my butt wasn't doing so great, either, although the soreness there resulted more from the hard seat. At least the steady breeze wafting across the water kept me from turning into a sweaty mess, and the streaky white clouds made cool patterns in the vibrant blue sky.

One nice thing about starting school at the butt-crack of dawn was that we got out early enough to enjoy the sunny afternoons, but now I worried it meant Cooper planned on going until nightfall, and I so wasn't going to make it.

"How long…" Row and a puff of air. "Do you usually…" Row, exhale. "Train for?"

"As long as possible," Copper replied from his spot in front of me, not even short of breath, which made me think he could go for a really, really long time.

Whoa, that came out wrong. Even though it'd only been in my head, I felt the need to mentally add that I meant rowing. Probably because I'd already accidentally admitted to noticing he was ripped, and that was *before* I saw the way the muscles in his arms and back moved as he worked those oars. He'd made that joke about what he could do with his ripped-ness, but seeing it in action…Well, I thought playing football showed off guys' muscles rather effectively, but rowing was a whole different ballgame.

Or a different *not ball* game, as it were. I snort-laughed at that thought, and then my breathing was off, and my oars slapped at the surface instead of gliding through the water like they needed to.

"We're getting off pace," Cooper said, the gruffness in his voice drifting over his shoulder.

"Yeah. Newsflash: I haven't done this for a while, and it was never a timed, race kind of thing." I gave up on pushing the oars through the water and hooked the ends of the handles under my arms, using them to rest on and catch my breath.

"Hmm." Cooper glanced at his watch. The watch I wanted to throw in the water, because he reset it and shouted out times every few minutes that meant nothing to me, but he didn't seem very happy with them, which made me feel like I was failing.

Who knew that someone who strolled around like they didn't have a care in the world could transform into someone so serious so quickly? He should time that attitude flip, because it was fast enough to win any race.

"I hoped we'd make better time," he said, and I fought the urge to flop onto the floor of the boat for a quick nap.

"Well, I hoped there'd be less rowing and more relaxing and getting a tan."

"That would hardly help me win the race."

With him facing forward, clearly he wasn't getting that I was only kidding—I mean I did hope that, but I definitely didn't expect it, and hello, if that were my main goal, I would've worn shorts. I didn't like not seeing his expressions, either, although now that he'd turned into Mr. Serious, it was probably better that way. "I wasn't talking strategy, I was talking wants, and it was supposed to be a joke."

Cooper finally spun enough for me to see his face, and his eyebrows were all scrunched up. "So you want to keep rowing?"

"I…" I blew my breath out past my lips, not caring that it made me sound like a horse. "I don't know how much longer I can go—I'm actually questioning if I can even make it back to the shore, or if I should just start praying for a strong wind to help you."

Cooper's all-business expression remained, and he glanced at the damn watch again.

I nudged his hip with the toe of my shoe. "I'll get faster and stronger, okay? It just might take me a week or so." I had a feeling it'd take longer than that, but I didn't want to kill any possible optimism that still might be hanging in the air, struggling to hold on to the idea that this might be fun.

"At least you don't weigh much," Cooper said.

"Thanks?"

"Actually, that might throw me off. If I get used to it, and then Jaden hops in, the extra weight will make us slower. Then again, he rows more effectively because of his years of experience, so…" I could practically see the wheels turning in his head.

"If you want, I can work up a story problem and then solve it so you can calculate exactly how much my weight and less experience will factor into your and his usual time." Strands of my hair swirled in front of my face and I swept them off, vowing to bring my backup hair-tie tomorrow. "Of course if I die of exhaustion out here, I won't be able to do it, and then I won't be able to help. Mathematically, or with training. Just saying."

Finally Cooper snapped out of it, his features softening. "I guess I shouldn't let you die of exhaustion the first day. I'll wait until right before Jaden is fully healed."

"How very noble of you."

He tipped his head and his dimples flashed in his cheeks. And then I might've checked out the muscles in his arms again, but only for a second—like a fraction of a second, really.

"You know, I didn't think this through," I said. "I pictured us facing each other. It feels like I'm hanging out with myself." *Well, myself and a super strong back, but I'm not going to focus on that, because it's weird and why do I keep thinking about it?*

Switching mental gears, I focused on the non eye-candy aspect. "But then I'd just have some mean rowing coach barking orders into my face."

Cooper arched an eyebrow. "'Mean,' huh?"

I nodded. "Now I know why I skipped this sport. It had nothing to do with my lack of coordination. It was the barked orders and pressure to row until your arms fall off."

"Whatever. You're way better at this than most girls. Most girls who don't have any training, anyway."

"Again, thanks?"

The boat wobbled as he spun around to face me. "No more hanging out with yourself. Or a coach who only wants to *challenge* you to score your best time."

I rolled my eyes, making the gesture nice and big so he knew I wasn't buying the no-pain, no-gain rhetoric.

Cooper gripped the oars and started rowing us back toward the shore.

I eyed the ends of my oars, but even the thought of grabbing them made my shoulders burn. "I'd offer to help, but my arms feel like noodles and I'm pretty sure you're going as fast without me as you did with me."

He gave a quick glance to his watch. "You help a little." I shook my head, but he simply grinned. "And keeping track of our beats and pacing will help a lot as we figure out which marks we need to hit in order to beat our previous times." With a jerk of his chin, he indicated the paper next to me, the one where I'd scribbled in the times and distance markers like he'd asked me to. "I want you to be as obsessive about that as you were about our history project—more so, if that's even possible."

"Oh, it is, and I'm going to make you regret saying that."

"Bring it," he said, his grin widening.

Maybe I should force him to sit facing the rear of the boat all the time, because the carefree fun Cooper was back. Intense, obsessed-with-time Cooper scared me a little, even while I liked seeing he was capable of that much passion in some aspects of his life.

The drive to improve his time was admirable, truly, but it also made me wonder what I'd gotten myself into with this deal.

I made a halfhearted attempt to help as I scanned the horizon. The sun now hung low in the sky, turning the shore opposite us into a contrast of dark, pine-tree-shaped spires and fiery sky. The stretched-out clouds glowed around the edges, and the oranges and golds reflected on the surface of the water. The boat and oars left ripples in the colored lake as we glided through it, leaving a trail someone could follow to find us, but only if they hurried, because it quickly faded.

With my exhaustion over having to constantly move through the water fading, a peaceful calm feeling overcame me. Maybe I occasionally missed Amber because it meant I rarely came to the lake anymore, which was especially hard when it'd felt like my second home that summer two years ago. Almost like my first home in some ways, because my real home at that time was bursting with sadness and hard to face.

The boat bumped the shore before I realized how close we were. I stood, planning on jumping onto the dirt and grass embankment so I could help pull the boat to shore. I nearly fell in the water but managed to land on a muddy spot instead, my shoes making a sloppy squishing sound.

When I grabbed the boat and tugged, it was heavier than I expected. My foot slipped, unable to get any traction in the slimy sludge, and I fell backward, all my momentum now working against me. As squishy as the mud was between my fingers, it sure was hard on the butt.

Cooper's laughter came out sputtered at first, like he'd made an attempt to stop it, but then he laughed full out, the boat rocking as he folded over. I flicked mud at him, but it barely hit his legs, which was hardly satisfying.

Once he semi-recovered from his laughing fit, he took a large step and jumped onto the dry part of the shore. *Show off.* He tugged the boat up next to him, then extended a hand to me.

"I like how you took care of the boat first," I grumbled as he grabbed my clean hand.

"Well, it doesn't have feet. It's hardly fair to expect *it* to climb onto the shore." His implication was clear—he expected *me* to have that ability. He yanked me up, and I nearly bumped into him. My hands automatically went to his waist.

He gripped my upper arms. "Whoa. You steady?"

Suddenly, I didn't feel steady at all. My stomach did a sommersault, and my skin tingled underneath his large, warm hands.

I must just be lightheaded from standing up so fast—that was it. I shook off the momentary dizziness, and glanced down. My muddy hand left a big smear of brown across his T-shirt and the top of his jeans. "Oh shoot, I got your clothes messy."

He shrugged and his voice came out low. "I don't mind getting dirty."

My gaze shot to his. Apparently I was the one with

muddy hands *and* dirty thoughts, but then dawning crossed his features.

"You thought I was giving you some line, didn't you?"

I shook my head. "No. Of course not."

"Mmm-hm. Guess you're not quite as serious as I thought." He tipped his head toward his truck. "C'mon. Let's get you home before the rest of your thoughts drift into the gutter and you offend my delicate sensibilities."

I opened my mouth to tell him he was the one who put them there, but luckily I stopped myself just in time. No way that wouldn't come out sounding inappropriate, and then he'd get the wrong idea and think I was crushing on him or something and run in the other direction.

That'd leave me with two social disasters on my hands, because I'd never pull off my goal to land Mick without Cooper by my side.

Chapter Seven

COOPER

I knocked on the door to Kate's house Friday night and then kicked a stray rock off the cement block that acted as their porch. We'd gone for our usual practice on the lake this afternoon, but right as we were getting into a good groove with our pacing, Dad called to remind me I was supposed to meet him at his office.

So we'd cut it short, and I was still reeling from the news that Dad arranged an internship for me with his firm over the summer when Kate called me in a panic. "It's been four days!" she'd shouted into the phone, loud enough I'd yanked it away from my ear. "And I still haven't even talked to Mick, and now it's the weekend…"

Honestly, after that, I didn't catch many more actual words. Let's just say she was freaking out.

So I'd offered to come over to talk strategy. It was better than dwelling on my planned-out future that was suddenly starting sooner than expected, and the suffocating feeling the internship news had brought on.

The guy standing in the yard next door bent over the hood of an RV, a tool in his hand, and I saw not just plumber's crack, but most of his grand canyon.

The door swung open. "Oh good, you're here." Kate grabbed my arm and yanked me inside so fast I almost tripped on the threshold. "I hope you have a plan, and this one better be more foolproof than your last one."

"You mean my one about starting a conversation with him?"

"Technically, that was my goal first, you know."

"And how's that working out for you?"

She threw up her hands. "It's not. I need more than you telling me to try to talk to him. I need the actual conversation fed to me."

"I hear that that's bad for you." I gave a dramatic sigh. "All empty calories, possible link to diabetes…"

She tilted her head and shot daggers at me. And she wondered why people assumed she was serious.

"I thought you were going to go with the football angle." We'd discussed as much yesterday on the lake.

"Yeah, but then I realized that'd work if, like, I'd just watched one of the games last weekend and could bring up what'd happened during it. But it's not football season anymore, and if I mention that I've seen him playing after school, doesn't that sound totally stalkerish?"

Oh, hell. She's giving me that deadly determined look. The one that says she wants me to actually answer. "Not if you word it right," I said, hoping I'd worded *my* response correctly. With her, questions I assumed were rhetorical weren't, and honest answers weren't always appreciated, either.

She ran a hand through her hair, switching the bulk of it to the other side. Several strands fell in her face and I had the urge to brush it back for her and see if it was as silky as it looked.

"It's just so hard to approach him when he's got all his friends around, or worse—all the girls," she said. "How is someone like me supposed to have a chance when every other girl in the school is practically throwing herself at him?"

"Because you're not like every other girl." I put my hands on her shoulders. She was wearing a tank top, and her skin was smooth and soft, and whatever perfume or soap she'd used smelled girly and awesome, and…delicious. That was the best way to describe it. So good I wanted to take a lick.

Clearly it's been too long since any girl threw herself at me.

I quickly dropped my hands. "But before he can see that, we have to get him to see you. That involves talking to him. Making him think about you." Man, this conversation was weird, and one I hoped I'd never have to have. Or, I guess more like I'd never known I would need to hope for that, but I definitely did now. "And I do have a plan for that."

She nodded over and over and some of the tension leaked out of her posture. "It's just that prom is only getting closer."

"I know."

"Which means we're on a tight deadline."

"I understand."

Her lips pressed together, the shimmery lip stuff on them drawing my attention for a moment before I snapped out of it. My focus was crap today. I blamed the bomb Dad dropped and the fact that it'd been a while since I'd kissed anyone. As soon as I got Pecker to notice Kate, I really needed to find a girl for myself. Hell, maybe I'd even go to prom.

I thought about the hoopla, from the tux with the matching vest or cumber-whatever-the-hell-it-was to the expectation of a fancy dinner and limo rides, and ruled it out. *No thanks.*

"But do you? Do you really?" Kate asked. "I don't think you understand how important this is to me. I feel like you think prom is just a silly dance."

She wasn't far off. "I get it, it's a rite of passage or whatever, but to me, it's more like…" *A big waste of time.* I didn't want to hurt her feelings, so I softened it to, "A lot of time and effort for one little night you'll barely remember in a few years."

Dealing with things like the big dance and other high school drama would only cut into time on the lake, and now I had even less of it. I'd fulfill my end of the bargain, but I wasn't going to let anything else get in the way.

Since Kate still looked concerned, I added, "But I understand that it's important to you, and I won't let you down, okay?"

"Okay," she said with a nod. She gestured over her shoulder. "Want a Dr Pepper? I was about to grab one."

"That'd be great, thanks." I followed her as she walked into a cozy kitchen that was vastly different from the large, ultra-modern one in my house—it was stainless steel and hanging pots over a massive granite island, all function. The decorations in this room had no rhyme or reason. A clock with colorful owls but no numbers sat over the stove, teacup-covered curtains hung over the window at the sink, and a wooden shelf held an assortment of ceramic figurines. Things like colorful roosters, cats, and a split in half Scooby Doo van. A closer glance revealed them to be salt and pepper shakers.

Every inch of the white fridge was covered in pictures, some newer ones of Kate and her mom, and some older of them with her dad. He wore Air Force fatigues in most, and several had him in his uniform. I knew he'd passed away a couple of years ago, right before Kate started at AA, but I didn't know enough to broach the topic.

The cool can Kate handed me felt nice against my palm, and the crack of the tab and hiss of the bubbles were all that filled the air for a moment.

When Kate pulled the tab on hers, she groaned. "Thanks

to the horrid training schedule you're forcing on me, even opening a soda hurts."

I grinned at her. "You love it."

"I love the lake. The rowing—especially the kind required to go fast—I could toss right in the water. I'd just watch it sink, happy as could be."

I put a hand over my heart like an arrow had hit me. "You wound me and my sport with your words."

Her laughter echoed through the colorful room. "You're too much." She took a swig of her soda and gestured toward the hallway. "My notebook's in my room. Let's go put together a full game plan for Operation Prom Date. I always feel better when I get my strategies down on paper."

I wondered if her dad used to speak in all military code, and if that was why she talked in terms like that and insisted on naming our operation. But again, it was above my clearance level. *Great. Now* I'm *doing it.*

The uniquely decorated kitchen had nothing on Kate's room. Bright blue paint on the walls, colorful paper lanterns hanging from the ceiling, and the black fan had white polka dots. A beaded curtain hung over her window, sending flashes of colored light around the room and across her dresser, where several framed pictures sat. The bursting-at-the seams bookshelf on the opposite side also had bigheaded figures lining the shelves. Oh, and a giant lizard wearing a tiny, yellow knitted scarf sat in the middle of her bed. It cocked its head at me, making the spiky parts on its neck stick out.

"That's Klaus," Kate said. "Don't worry, he's got a much better temperament than his namesake."

"Oh? And who is he named after?"

"An original vampire. From the show *The Originals*? Technically he was on *The Vampire Diaries* first, but they did a spin off, and anyway…" She scooped up the creature as she sat on her bed. "Klaus kills for fun—the vampire. This Klaus is too lazy to do much of anything."

I sat next to her on the bed, still taking in her collection of figurines.

"That's my Funko Pop collection. I paired them up the way they should be on the shows." She gestured at one in a green hood and the blond figure next to him with the glasses. I realized it was from *Arrow*.

"I ship Olicity the hardest."

"'Ship' them?"

"I want them in a relationship. Like I'd put them in a ship together so they'd be forced to see they're perfect for each other, bribe the writers to get them together, ship them. Partnership, friendship, *please-God*-put-them-in-a-relationship-already ship them."

"Oh-kay."

"It's a common phrase. Oliver and Felicity are totally my OTP, which means one true pairing, if you haven't somehow heard of that, either. I also ship Alexa and Clarke on *The 100* a crazy amount, and I was pretty mad at the writers for a while, but something happened and…well, I won't spoil it, but I *might've* teared up. Then of course there's Stydia and Captain Swan"—she pointed at a blond figure wearing a red jacket and a goateed dude with a hook for a hand—"I used to be all about Damon and Elena, but there toward the end, I shipped her and a coffin. Which sounds mean, I know, but vampires don't technically die, so a bit nicer?"

"I'm still judging you too much for saying 'ship them the hardest' to judge you for the vampire stuff."

She smacked my arm and I laughed. Honestly, I was also trying to keep up with all the words she'd spouted, trying to make sense of them. We'd spent the past few afternoons on the boat, and the more time I spent with her, the more amused I was by her, even though I only understood about half of what she said.

Klaus crawled higher on her lap and she rubbed his chin. I never knew a lizard could smile, but damned if the thing didn't grin. Kate caught my eye. "Just call me Khaleesi, mother of dragons. Or dragon, as it were. Please tell me you at least get that reference."

"*Game of Thrones*. I've only read the first book, though. Okay, half of the first book, but I meant to pick it back up. But then I sort of just watched the show instead."

She glanced around like someone might be listening and then leaned in. "Don't tell anyone, but I've never read the books."

I leaned a few inches closer, until I could see the different shades of green in her eyes. "Your secret is safe with me."

"You're starting to have a lot of my secrets, so I certainly hope so."

Unexpected warmth swirled through my chest. I'd never thought I would want to be a secret keeper, but there was something about having Kate's trust that made me proud to be one.

She pulled out a notebook and my tingly happy vibes faded a bit when I saw the outlined list, *Operation Prom Date* written across the top. Which was stupid, because that was why I'd come over.

The same organizational skills that had me inwardly groaning now had come in handy during the past few days of training, just like I'd guessed they would. She'd even done some calculations on how much faster we'd have to row to beat our previous times, even though she also joked she should hide them from me so I wouldn't "get all crazy and practically kill us" trying to do better.

"Okay, so for reals, I'm going to talk to him this week." She tapped the end of her pen to her still-shimmery lip. The same full lip I shouldn't be noticing. But when I dropped my gaze, all I got was an eyeful of her legs—their crossed position made her shorts hike up higher on her thighs and now I was thinking about those. "Cooper?"

I jerked my head up and swallowed. "You talk to him. Say hi or whatever. Bring up football if you want. But you're gonna need something more to really set your plan into motion." I racked my brain for an idea, one that would work, because I needed to stop thinking thoughts I shouldn't. "We need to do something big."

Chapter Eight

KATE

The "something big" hung in the air, more intimidating by the second. Cooper seemed to be deep in thought, that little crease between his eyebrows that formed when he went into Mr. Serious mode on the lake showing up. I didn't dare interrupt, hoping genius had just struck. Especially if it was the kind of genius that'd help me not feel like such a failure when it came to my prom plans.

I also hoped it wouldn't be scary. Big sounded scary. Plus, like I said, Mr. Serious face, and that usually meant barked orders.

Finally his gaze returned to the present day and my room. "There's a party tomorrow night. You're going to go with me. And we're going to act like…"

I'd never liked cliffhangers, not on my TV shows, not in books—especially when the sequel's release date was months to years away—and definitely not in my real-world conversations. "Like what?"

"Like we came together, but not as a couple. As in a casual thing." He ran his hand over his jaw and then rubbed the back of his neck. "Do you think you can do that?"

The amount of oxygen I took in thinned and my gut tightened. "So I'd go with you and just play it cool?"

"Yeah. But also, I might put my arm around you, or stand really close. Maybe make it look like we could be more than friends, but not like we're in a relationship."

"That seems like a very odd limbo to be in." I frowned at the idea of being tugged around like that, thinking a guy was into me, only to find out he acted like that with other people, too. But that was what everyone did these days, right? It certainly fit in with Mick's usual MO. He and the girls he "dated" were together one night, not the next. Sometimes they were even hanging on other people or kissing them in the halls within the same week.

"We can try to think of another way if you'd be uncomfortable," Cooper said.

"No." I put my hand on his arm, vaguely noticing it was, in fact, as firm as it looked when I sat behind him every day on the lake. "I'm overthinking, as usual. It's just pretend, so it's not like it matters."

He nodded. "Just pretend. Once we take some of that serious edge off, then guys will see you as the easygoing chick they'd like to take to a party."

"And then to *the* party." I needed to hear the end result, because the part of me I didn't realize was so opinionated hated the thought of people thinking I skipped from guy to guy so easily.

Eyes on the prize. I just need Mick to see me first. I'm sure if he met the right person he'd want more, and that person's going to be me. This is the way we'll be able to get to know each other and get to that point.

I pulled my notebook to me and scribbled "Mick and I

go to prom together" in giant letters. Staring at them helped soothe my nerves.

Then I looked up at Cooper, whose hazel eyes were fixed on me. That made another calming wave rush over me. It wasn't like it'd be hard to act like I found Cooper attractive. Flirting with him would be almost natural, like how natural it was for my mom with complete strangers. Maybe I needed a guy I trusted on the other end of my pretend flirting, but practice made perfect, right? In no time, I'd be managing it with the guy who rendered me incapable of speech with one of his sexy smirks. Or you know, by simply looking my way.

"Let's do it," I said.

With that out of the way, I figured we could get on with our Friday night. I flipped my notebook closed and tossed it aside.

"So that's that?" Cooper asked.

"For now." I glanced at the time. I hardly ever had plans on the weekend. Even Mom had gone out tonight— I'd practically had to shove her out the door, but I knew she needed nights out with her friends. She was more of an extrovert than I was. As much as she accidentally flirted, she never dated. For her sake, I wanted her to move on, but for mine, I was glad I hadn't had to deal with it yet. I wasn't ready for some strange guy to come in and change everything; to make that feeling of Dad never living here again that much more permanent. "Did you have somewhere else you needed to be?"

"Need? No."

Ever since the pretend-we're-more-for-the-party discussion, the vibe had turned a bit weird, and I wanted back the easy one Cooper and I normally shared. "We could watch a movie or something? But if you've got more exciting plans, or—"

"I'm down for a movie." One corner of his mouth kicked

up, way too mischievousness in the curve. "But I get to choose it."

My fingers curled around my remote protectively. "Giving out movie choosing privileges isn't something I do lightly."

"Well, I don't hang out with the Mother of Dragons lightly. Especially when the dragon's been giving me dirty looks for the past five minutes."

I looked down at Klaus, who did look quite disgruntled about not getting all my attention. "Down, boy. Wait to blast him with fire until we hear what movie he's going to make us sit through."

Hesitantly, I extended the remote.

Cooper took it from me, his callused fingers brushing mine, and the vibe changed again, this time more electrically charged. Which had to be a mix of anticipation and anxiety over what movie he'd pick—yeah, that was definitely why my stomach crawled up to kiss my ribcage.

He scrolled through the options, pausing on movies I planned on protesting against a few times, only to move on. The cover for *Terminator: Salvation* filled the screen. "This was what I was thinking."

"I haven't seen it."

"I think you'll like it. And I'm saying that as your trusted secret keeper."

"I guess we won't roast him quite yet," I said to my bearded dragon, who simply stared at me. I glanced at Cooper and thought about asking if he'd add the fact that I talked to my pet to my secret list, but figured it was understood. Not to mention awkward to bring up in the first place.

I stood and put Klaus in his cage, tossing in extra food before settling next to Cooper again.

He'd been texting someone, but I didn't see who and was doing my best not to be nosey. He pocketed his phone, leaned back on the headboard next to me, and hit play…

About thirty minutes in, I went to shift and groaned. Usually I tried to stifle sounds like that, but I couldn't help it. "Everything hurts whenever I move."

"So don't move," Cooper said, as if never moving again was an effective, realistic solution for having muscles so sore you wanted to cry.

"Does that mean I don't have to be at practice tomorrow, coach?"

That got his full attention. "Oh, you'll be at practice, and if you complain, I'll make you drop and give me twenty."

"I couldn't even do one push up, much less twenty."

"Then I guess you better be at practice."

I stuck out my lips, not above pouting if it'd give me one day of rest. "But I'll need time for party prep."

"We'll row at noon and go for a couple of hours. That gives you plenty of time to prep."

I let my head fall back against the headboard and gave a dramatic fake cry. "I need a day off. My muscles need a break, or by the time we get to the party, I'll just be crying every time I move, and that doesn't seem like a very casual, cool thing to do." When he didn't immediately give in, I brought my hands into prayer position, despite the pain it caused. "Please, please have mercy on my muscles and give me a break, Coach Grouchy Pants."

His brow furrowed. "Fine. But Sunday at noon, your ass better be on the lake."

I saluted him, then groaned again, because it hurt my arm, which only made him laugh. Smacking his arm made pain shoot through my shoulder, but it was worth it.

I expected him to launch into a cheesy sports speech about pain and gain, but instead, he handed me the pillow he'd been using. "I'm tough enough to not need any sissy cushions."

"That's because your body is used to all the rowing."

He shot me a sidelong glance, the colors from the TV dancing across his features. "My ripped body?"

"If it wouldn't hurt, I'd smack you again." I added the pillow on top of the one cushioning my back. Obviously Cooper was super scared, because when I twisted back around, he waggled his eyebrows. "Okay, adding the eyebrows just bumped you up to a nine on the Kanye Douchebag Scale. I should've never told you that you got ripped. It went right to your head."

"Oh, I already knew." He cracked a grin and put his hands behind his head as a rest, his elbows out to the side, creating the picture-perfect image of *relaxed, confident dude*. Who was, in fact, ripped.

I crossed my ankles, glad at least my legs functioned without pain. "I like this movie and all, but there's not really a couple for me to ship. Unless we're talking shipping me and him, because talk about ripped."

Cooper shook his head. "Are you one of those people who talk through movies?"

"When it's not one of mine, yes. Otherwise, I do sometimes talk, but mostly just to Klaus, who completely agrees."

"Naturally."

I laughed, but did my best to be quiet through the rest of the movie. I thought nothing was as good as an empty weekend stretched before me, lots of hours to binge watch. But having Cooper watching with me? Well, a girl could get used to that.

Although, not really. As soon as Mick and I got together, I probably wouldn't have as much time for hanging out like this. A twinge of sorrow went through me, and I told myself to stop being overdramatic about something that hadn't even happened.

The sound of the door opening broke through the music that accompanied the credits rolling up the screen.

"Sounds like my mom is home," I said.

Cooper shot up, his back stick straight. "Will she be upset that I'm in your bedroom?"

I hadn't really thought about it, and it wasn't like I had a lot of experience with boys in my room, but I couldn't see her caring. "Nah. If anything, she'll be surprised. We should really shock her. Put your hand on my knee and we'll act like we were just making out."

Cooper couldn't look more horrified by the prospect, which made me worry we'd never be able to pull off tomorrow night's plan. I tried to smother the offense that automatically drifted up because I was only joking and had my sights set on someone else anyway. But would it kill him to act like the idea wasn't totally repulsive? My confidence with boys was shaky enough as it was.

"Kate?" Mom called. "I'm home, and I have some crazy stories for you. I have no idea what's wrong with guys these days. Nadine's doing the online dating thing, and she's already had three guys send her pics of their—"

"I have company!" I shouted before Mom could finish. Judging from the heat in my cheeks and the flush in Cooper's, it was too late to avoid veering into awkward territory. So much for shocking her—she definitely got the jump on that.

Mom stopped in the doorway. She was flushed as well, but more in the way that meant she'd had a few drinks and had done some dancing. "Oh. Hey, Kate's company." Her eyebrows scrunched up as she glanced from me to Cooper, and then back to me. Then she beamed at him like he was a puppy, and she hoped I'd keep him. Clearly she'd had too much to drink to be subtle.

"Mom, this is my friend Cooper. Cooper Callihan."

"Callihan." She pressed her lips together. "Your father's a lawyer, right?"

"Yes, ma'am," Cooper said, his usual light-heartedness

gone. Almost like he thought Mom might interrogate him or perhaps ask him for legal advice.

"Please don't call me ma'am. Makes me feel old. Call me Melanie. Or is that improper? I never know what the damn rules are with that kind of thing. I suppose I could settle for Ms. Hamilton, but I'd still prefer Melanie." She swung her arm, and I noticed her heels were in her hand instead of on her feet. "Anyway, you guys have fun. But not *too* much fun."

"Thanks, Mom. Good night."

She tapped the door. "I feel like I should say something parental, like this stays open. At least until we can discuss this *friendship* more." She winked at me and giggled. Then her expression turned as serious as she could get it under the circumstances. "I'm not usually like this, or even drunk at all, I swear."

"Remember to put aspirin and a glass of water by your bed. In fact, you should probably take one now."

"Good idea." Mom's smile widened. "I love having a smart daughter who thinks ahead." Her gaze moved to Cooper. "Which is why I'm a tad protective of her. Just so you know." She stage-whispered. "See? I can totally pull off being all mom-like."

"You're definitely rocking the mom thing right now," I said with a laugh, while also wishing she'd hurry and go to bed before she said anything else.

With a final wave, she was gone.

"Okay, I thought my mom wasn't very embarrassing, but that…" I placed a hand on my cheek, hoping it didn't look as pink as the heat radiating from it suggested. "Well, that was embarrassing."

"It's kind of nice, actually. I can see how much you guys care about each other." Cooper stood. "I better get going." He squeezed my shoulder, and while it made my sore muscles scream a little, the zips of energy counteracted it enough to make me want him to do it again. "Thanks for the movie."

"Thanks for helping me with my operation."

"Right. The Operation. Of course." He lowered his hand, his fingertips dragging down my arm. "I'll pick you up for the party tomorrow at seven. Since we're going big, you might want to wear something a little bolder and flashier than usual." Once he reached the doorway, he paused and glanced back at me. "But if you change your mind, we don't have to go through with the plan. Just putting that out there."

Dad and I used to go on missions all the time together. Like while we were shopping, he'd tell me to keep an eye out for a guy with a fedora—he wasn't to be trusted. And we'd look until we found some random guy who had one on and plot our plan of attack. Not real attack, of course. But our hypothetical operations were detailed and epic.

Then there were the real ones, like cleaning the house as fast as we could before my mom came home, or surprising her with dinner, or buying her the perfect present for her birthday.

Real or fake, we used military lingo and acted as if our lives depended on our success. This entire operation brought back some of those good memories and the rush of making a plan of attack, and like back then, failure wasn't an option. So bold, flashy clothes and attending a party where I pretended to be a little more than friends with Cooper? I could totally handle that.

"I won't change my mind," I said.

Chapter Nine

KATE

With the help of my friends Advil and IcyHot, I was able to push past the soreness in my muscles and curl my hair. In a few more weeks, my arms better be super toned from all the rowing.

I also watched a tutorial on eyeliner, and after several failed experiments at "wings" I went for more of a smoky eye. After so many smudged layers of black eyeliner, it was really my only choice. But I decided it worked.

The red dress I took from Mom's closet was too over-the-top. There was bold and flashy, and then there was trying way too hard. It wasn't me, either. I wanted to be me, but like me 2.0. The blue sleeveless top with the beaded sheer overlay fit my goal, especially when paired with my tightest jeans with the cute zippers on the front. On the way out the door, I added another spritz of perfume and slipped my new, strawberry-flavored-yet-still-shimmery lip-gloss into my pocket.

Mom whistled as I walked through the living room. After

being dressed up last night, she was doing the super chill thing, wearing yoga pants and a T-shirt, and about to dig into ice cream while she did some binge watching of her own. "You going out with Cooper again?"

"We never went out, so I can't do it again, now can I?"

Mom stuck a bite of Chunky Monkey in her mouth. "You've been spending a lot of time with him this week."

"Because we're friends."

"Because you still have a crush on that cute football player?"

I wobbled my head back and forth, unsure whether to answer that. "I'm just taking it a day at a time." And those days were going to add up quick, so I needed tonight to make a difference. I had maybe two more weeks before he lined up another date, if it wasn't too late already.

Oh no, what if he has a date already? This will all be for nothing. I sucked in a breath and let it out, telling myself I would've heard about it. Whisperings about prom were starting, but going by last year's timeline, things got real in the next few weeks. I still had a chance.

"Well, that Cooper boy is super cute if you ask me."

"He's super cute if you ask most anyone. His cuteness does not negate the fact that we're just friends. He's not interested in being more."

Mom leaned forward as if she were about to glean some big gossip. "But if he was, you would be?"

The doorbell rang. "Saved by the bell. We'll talk crushes later."

"I'm holding you to that." She extended a scoop of ice cream toward me. "For the road?"

I ate it off the spoon, not quite prepared for the size or the cold. Then I hugged Mom good-bye and went to answer the door.

Cooper stood on the other side, and the cute descriptor

entered my head again, because dang, the guy was nice on the eyes. His curls were more tamed than usual, and he had on a dark blue button down. The sleeves were rolled up so that his forearms were exposed, and suddenly I found myself unable to look away from that strong line, wondering if it'd always been there, and kicking myself for not taking time to appreciate it before.

"Damn," he said, then his gaze moved over my shoulder to Mom and a slightly panicked look hit his eye.

"Don't worry, I'm sure she didn't hear you swear," I whispered.

"Actually, I did," she called out. "But since it's because he's simply admiring your beauty, I'll damn well let it slide."

"Bye, Mom!" I pulled the door closed behind me and hoped the cool night air would help calm the heat in my face.

"You look nice," he said.

"Am I bold and flashy enough, though?"

He looked me up and down, and my stomach followed along, rising and dipping. "You're all the things," he said, and his voice came out low and slightly gruffer than usual, which made my stomach dip all over again.

I grinned at him. "Thanks. You look nice as well."

The dimple in his cheek flashed. "Am I tall and ripped enough, though?"

"So, so much regret," I joked as I hooked an arm through his. After all, we were about to pretend to be closer than we were. Might as well get a little bit used to it.

He opened the passenger door of his truck, and before stepping out of the way, he leaned in close and inhaled. "You smell nice, too."

Goose bumps scattered across my skin. Luckily he was already rounding the hood, so hopefully he didn't notice. I needed to stop noticing. This night was about the cute football player. The cute rower acted like touching my knee and pretending we'd been making out would be appalling just last night.

The more I thought about it, the surer I became that my nerve wires were just getting crossed because I related hanging out with Cooper with landing Mick, who I'd liked for-freakin'-ever. *Of course* I got tingly surges.

Extra bright side? The things Cooper noticed about me would be the things Mick would also notice. Hopefully. *Boys all pretty much work the same, right?*

Resolve filled me and I straightened so I wouldn't smash my hair. *Mick Pecker, here I come. I hope you're ready for me.*

Chapter Ten

COOPER

I shouldn't have sniffed her neck like some weirdo. Even in the cab of my truck I could smell her perfume, that scent I'd noticed last night. Lately, I was noticing way too much. At least she had on jeans tonight, although I could easily recall the way her legs looked in those tiny shorts yesterday, and her pants were tight enough I could still see the shape of them, and I *might've* checked out her ass as I'd walked her to my truck.

What the hell was wrong with me?

A sweet girl asks me to help her land a guy and suddenly I'm ogling her and thinking about her lips and her perfume and her legs and—*man*, I needed to derail this line of thought.

So I focused on the way the headlights lit up the narrow road and trees flanking it, and my plan to put her on Pecker's radar tonight. For all I knew this attempt would crash and burn and I'd discover I knew nothing about people my age. Hell, maybe I should suggest everyone go outside and stare at the stars once we arrived at the party. Just really drive it home that I didn't know what it took to be cool, only that not caring had somehow made me cooler.

"You okay?" Kate asked.

I kept my eyes on the road to keep my head in the game. "Yeah. I was just thinking about the lake."

"When are you *not* thinking about the lake?"

I smiled at her, and she smiled back, and a sensation I hadn't felt in a long time went through my gut. "Not to rub it in, but you missed out today. There was this perfect breeze and enough cloud cover to keep the temperature nice and cool. You wouldn't have been able to get your sought-after tan, of course."

"Well, then, I'm out. Do you think I'm doing this whole rowing training for my health?"

No. You're doing it for some meathead who only thinks about himself. I needed to remember that before my brain got any other ideas and I did something stupid that'd ruin the easy, fun thing we had going on.

"It's always a bit crowded on the weekends, but it wasn't too bad today." The lake. That'd keep me safe. Whenever I thought about veering from the plan, I'd throw out more facts about it. Remind myself that I needed her help with training there, in addition to the side fun we were having.

"Maybe we should just wait until Monday to train more, then."

I scowled at her and she held up her hands.

"Just kidding, Coach Grouchy Pants. I'm so excited to get out on the lake with you tomorrow that I can hardly control myself. Your jaw is totally going to drop once you see the time we make."

"It better," I said, keeping my tone light. Calling me a grouchy pants was hardly fair. More like clinging to every hour of fun and freedom before a decade of boredom and falling in line. I almost told her about the internship, simply because it'd be nice to vent, but that'd be a total downer, and we had enough to think about tonight if we were going to pull off our plan.

Kate scooted forward as we pulled up to the two-story cabin with as many cars as trees. "Wait. Who's throwing the party?"

"Paris."

Her shoulders deflated. "Great. She haaates me."

"How could anybody hate you?"

"I don't know, yet people pull it off. Basically I wouldn't be her lackey, but she was cool enough that Amber didn't mind, and maybe I don't exactly have kind feelings for her because of that, either."

"As you can see, half the school is here. You can avoid her easy enough."

"Right." Kate nodded and reached for her door handle. Then she abruptly spun around, her face pale. "Remind me why I'm doing this again."

"Because I'm a genius and you trust me completely." I figured joking would be better than having to say the truth out loud. For one, thinking about being this weird dating puppet master made me seriously reconsider my life choices, and for two, irritation started to rise up when I thought of Pecker in general.

"I do trust you, and you are a genius." Kate ran her palms down her jeans. "But I'm, like, crazy nervous. Way more nervous than I thought I'd be."

"Just relax. I'll be right there with you—"

"With your arm around me, acting all flirty, and like we're casual acquaintances who probably fool around a little?"

Whatever you do, do not *think about what it might be like to fool around a little.* I ninja chopped away the image of pulling her close. "Yeah, that's the vibe we're going for. But like I said, I'm not going to be super possessive or anything."

"What about…kissing?"

Every ounce of my restraint went to keeping myself from looking at her lips, and I quickly shut down all thoughts of sparkly lip gloss and driving my hand through her hair to satisfy my curiosity about how it'd feel between my fingers. "I don't think that'll be necessary. Maybe on the cheek? Like when I whisper it's time to go? And you'll act like you're…" *Into it.* That was what I meant, but I worried it'd come out wrong and only make her more nervous—not to mention rev me up more—so I softened it. "Like you think that sounds like a great idea."

She nodded again and again, like she did when her nervousness reached the next level.

I took her hand and slipped my fingers between hers. "We don't have to do this."

She looked at me, blinking the green eyes that looked even bigger and brighter thanks to the makeup she'd put on. "No, I want to."

Could've fooled me. "Okay. I'm going to open the truck door and pull you out with me."

I wrapped my fingers around the plastic handle.

"Wait," she said before I tugged.

I turned back to her. "You're doing this for your crazy mission thing, and as you like to remind me, you're on a tight deadline. It'll work. But first we have to go inside that party and pull off step one."

"I think this is step two." Her eyes met mine. "And call it by its name."

"Why?"

"Because it'll make me feel better." She sunk her teeth into her bottom lip. "Please?" How could I possibly say no to her sweet features and that pleading look that said she really needed this.

I sighed, drawing it out, because I might be the sucker in this situation, but it didn't mean I'd completely own it. "Operation Prom Date is officially go for launch. Once this mission is complete, we'll report to home base for further instructions."

A smile spread across her face and she tightened her grip on my hand. "Okay. Now I'm ready."

Chapter Eleven

KATE

By now, Cooper most likely considered me certifiable, but he went along with it. I'm not sure why it was more reassuring to hear "Operation Prom Date" coming from his lips. Probably because he had a nice voice, deep and a bit husky. Plus, "crazy mission thing" *made* me feel crazy, which hampered the confidence I would need to play the role of *friend who imbibed in ambiguous levels of benefits with one of her guy friends.*

In fact, in the past week, Cooper had somehow become my closest friend. Maybe that was sad, but sad seemed like the wrong word to use when it came to spending time with Cooper. *A good jump-start to trying to make friends once I hit college, maybe?* As if he knew I needed it, Cooper gave my hand an extra squeeze as we walked into the party.

But then he dropped it.

Holding hands was too possessive, apparently. Still, I missed the lifeline immediately, my nerves replacing the calm

I'd possessed for a whole minute or so.

"Hey, Coop," someone said, and Cooper reached out and fist bumped him.

The noise of the party overwhelmed me, so many conversations going on at once. Music blared through the room, too, the bass line vibrating the frames on the wall and working its way under my skin, until my heart beat in time with it.

Within minutes, it was clear that Cooper knew everyone.

And that everyone didn't know me. I received a lot of blank looks with a few occasional finger points as they worked to remember my name or why I looked familiar.

"This is Kate," Cooper said, draping his arm over my shoulders.

"Oh yeah," Kevin Miller said. "We had Spanish class together last semester, right?"

Wrong. But saying so seemed rude—not to mention on the uptight side of the scale—so I gave a noncommittal shrug.

Gradually we made our way through the party, room by room. There were lots of familiar faces, but honestly, I didn't remember how I knew them or all of their names, so I told myself it was fine they didn't know who I was.

"I'm guessing this is my replacement?" a guy from our left asked, his brown eyes on me. He had tawny skin, dark hair that looked like it might be curly if he'd let it grow out, and an open and warm grin. I noticed the splinted wrist and put two and two together—because math was my thing.

"Jaden, this is Kate, your temporary replacement," Cooper said. "Kate, Jaden Kelekolio, the guy who gets drunk and falls out of trees like a dumbass."

"Hey, it was a graceful fall, thank-you-very-much. At least a nine, nine point two." Jaden extended his left hand and I fumbled to shake it, the opposite hand thing throwing me off for a second.

"Keleko-what?" I worried I'd butcher it if I didn't put it in my memory for good—and still might no matter how hard I tried—and suddenly I understood why he was one of the few dudes Cooper referred to by first name.

"Kelekolio. It's Polynesian, and I've found very few people can pronounce it, so don't worry, there won't be a quiz later. Jaden works, or some of my teammates call me JK, so I respond to that as well." A group of people pushed past, and Jaden curled his injured arm tighter to his body as he scooted closer to me. "So, Kate, I just have to ask…does Callihan get all scary intense with you on the water, too?"

I mirrored his conspiratorial posture. "Only every second we're out there. I thought it was because I was a beginner, and that I must just be royally screwing up on everything."

"Nah, he's always like that when it comes to rowing. You should've seen him in our eight-man team."

Cooper frowned. "Hey. I'm not that bad. I tell you guys good job, too."

"Must've been when I was too delirious and exhausted to hear it," I said, and Jaden snorted a laugh.

Cooper's frown deepened, and I nudged him with my elbow. "It's okay. I think I speak for Jaden when I say we're just honored to be in the presence of such rowing greatness." I put my hand on my heart, over-the-top dramatic, and sighed.

"Watch it," Cooper said, and he poked me in the side, making me jerk as a squeal escaped my lips. He turned to Jaden. "Maybe you can come out with us sometime? Give newbie here a few tips as we drag your dead weight around? Even if some of them include how to deal with me."

"Sure thing, man."

A gorgeous girl with big brown eyes, long wavy black hair, and an hourglass figure I couldn't help envy a little bit, walked up to Jaden. Their features were similar enough that I guessed they were related, but didn't say so in case they were dating—making things awkward was a specialty of mine, but I was trying to give it up.

"Can we go already?" she asked.

"Kate, meet Alana, my twin sister who's so serious that I worried she'd forgotten how to have fun, so I had to talk her into coming, mostly because driving one handed is trickier than it sounds. Clearly, though, I was right about her penchant for misery—she's even farther gone than I thought." He put his hand on her forehead, and she slapped it away as he laughed.

She turned to me and gave me a warm smile. "Hello, Kate. Usually I'm nicer—" Jaden snorted and she glared daggers at him. "*But* this isn't my scene, and I'm over it."

"I get that," I said. "It's not usually my scene, either. I'm trying something new."

Jaden eyed her, his expression saying *See? Try it out.*

She stumbled forward as someone bumped into her from behind. She spun around and glared at the bad boy of the football team, Vance Mitchell, a junior with long hair and a longer rap sheet from what I heard. "Excuse you."

"Sorry," he slurred. "These guys…" He got distracted with blatantly checking Alana out, and dawning crossed his features. "Hey, you're my new neighbor. Why don't I get you a drink and welcome you properly?"

"I have a boyfriend."

"I have a goldfish," he said, and all of us looked at him like he might be crazy—clearly he and alcohol didn't mix so well. But then a huge grin spread across his face. "Oh. I thought we were talking about stuff that didn't really matter."

She shook her head and turned back to Jaden. "I'm going home." She clamped on to his uninjured arm. "And since you're all incapacitated, you're coming with me."

With a sigh, Jaden started after her. "Catch you later, Coop. Kate."

Cooper nodded and nudged me toward the kitchen. "Okay, time to get this mission back on track." When we reached the keg, he poured me a cup. Then he leaned close, his hand going to my lower back. "You don't have to drink it, but at least hold it and take an occasional sip."

I peered up at him. Of course I knew he was tall, but with his body almost pressed against me, I had to crane my neck even more. "And if I do want to drink?"

"Go for it. I'll stay sober and cut you off before you get drunk enough to do something stupid."

"Oh, if you want to see impressive, I can make a fool of myself completely sober."

A smile curved Cooper's lips and his dimples showed up full-force. He brushed the section of hair that'd fallen over my left eye off my face and tucked it behind my ear.

Time froze while my heart jolted into motion. I'd seen the gesture countless times in TV shows and movies, and while it always gave me butterflies, experiencing it first-hand made them a hundred times more intense.

His fingers spread on my back and he pressed me closer. His lips lowered to my ear, and his warm breath skated across my neck. "Mick's nearby. Now might be a good time to giggle like I said something funny and attract a bit of attention."

Sure. If my brain could catch up and overtake the hazy sensation that Cooper's touch had brought on. I'd like to blame it on the alcohol, but I hadn't had so much as a sip.

I leaned into him, careful not to crush the cup between us, and ran a finger down his chest. "Can't you just say something funny, so my giggle doesn't come out fake sounding?" I whispered.

"Why'd the chicken cross the road?"

I grinned up at him, grateful he played along so easily. "I don't know."

"I don't know, either. You're the one who asked for a joke

on the spot."

I laughed, and it came out louder than I expected, but completely genuine. That made Cooper laugh, and that made me laugh even harder. With that victory coursing through me, I scanned the room for Mick.

He was actually looking my way, a puzzled expression on his face. And I wasn't sure where it came from, but I winked at him.

His eyebrows arched, and I flashed him a coy smile. Then I turned back to Cooper, needing him to tell me what move to make next before I lost all the ground I'd gained.

Cooper slid his arm around my waist, hooking his hand on my hip, and slowly turned us so we were both facing Mick. He gave him the nod, that casual guy gesture I could never pull off. "Hey, man."

"'Sup, Callihan. You getting ready for the Spring Festival Boat Race? I know I am."

Cooper tensed but he hid it well—if I weren't plastered against his body, I probably wouldn't have been able to tell. "I'm more focused on keeping up my training for college. You know how it is."

"I do," Mick said, that sexy smirk on his face. Then his attention moved to me, and my heart skipped a beat. "Hey, Kate. I don't usually see you at these parties."

O-M-G, he knows my name! I'll just die happy right now and call it good.

"She's usually at the Manchester parties," Cooper filled in, most likely when he realized I'd become incapable of speech. "I finally convinced her to come to this one with me." He jostled me, which I took to mean, say something so we can cross off your damn "talk to Mick" bullet point.

"What can I say? Those Manchester peeps throw some good parties." Did my voice come out casual and cool? Or did I ruin it by throwing in the word "peeps"? *Don't think about that, or you'll* definitely *ruin it.* "I hear the ones up at the University of New Hampshire are pretty fun, so I've been meaning to drive up to Concord and check them out. Isn't that one of the places where you might play football?"

His eyes lit up. "They offered me a spot, yeah. I might have to hit you up for your thoughts on going there versus the other universities I'm looking at. The coaches are all on me for a decision. It's a lot of pressure, and I don't want to choose wrong."

I nodded, and then I nodded some more. *He knows my name. He wants my thoughts on UNH. I can totally do tons of research, and then I'll have the perfect conversation starter.*

As long as he doesn't expect me to talk about it tonight.

Holy crap, what if he wants to talk about it tonight? I'm so unprepared.

Cooper curled me to him. "Need another refill?"

"I think I've got a little more left in this one." I lifted the drink I hadn't touched yet to my lips. It took everything in me to not show how disgusting I found it. I couldn't believe people were downing this nasty beer like it was soda.

Silence crept into the air, the conversation stilting as I struggled to come up with something more to say.

Cooper slipped his hand into my back pocket. Shock and a zing of awareness shot through me. I was pretty sure some offense should be mixed in there, too, because hello, his hand was on my butt! "Catch you later, man," he said.

"Yeah." Mick's blue, blue eyes moved to me. "Later, Kate."

"For sure." I added a weird finger wave that I meant to be flirty but was fairly certain came across as creepy. I supposed it'd be greedy to ask for more than five minutes of normalcy.

"Sorry for the ass grab," Cooper said as soon as we stepped into the living room, where people were getting louder and sloppier by the second. "He was just staring, and you seemed to be stuck on what to say, and I...I just reacted."

"Oh. It's...fine. I'm casual, cool Kate, remember?" I bumped my shoulder into his since he looked a bit worried. "I mean, I'm a little concerned that your knee-jerk reaction is ass grabbing. I'm guessing you're either very popular or very unpopular with your rowing teammates."

A crooked grin spread across his face. "Depends on the teammate."

"So now we...?"

Cooper glanced around. A guy was currently standing on the coffee table, waving his cup around as he talked. Beer sloshed onto the floor, and he was one wrong move from falling, but no one seemed very concerned, including Cooper. Apparently this kind of thing happened all the time. *How dare those imaginary parties with Manchester peeps leave me so unprepared!*

"Circulate a bit," Cooper said, "make sure you're in Pecker's orbit at least one more time—although this time, barely acknowledge him. After that, we'll make our exit, leaving everyone to wonder will they or won't they."

Wow. It was one thing to talk about having all of our classmates speculating on the status of our hooking up, but being here now, with several of them looking at us with inquisitive glances, made it super real.

I returned my attention to Cooper and swallowed. I was already pretty deep into this whole facade. What was a little more pretending?

Chapter Twelve

COOPER

I don't know what I was thinking slipping my hand into Kate's back pocket like that. Despite doing my best to not totally cop a feel while I pulled off the fake move, the way it'd curved nicely against my palm remained burned in my memory. Even more disturbing, I couldn't stop thinking about how much I liked being able to pull her to me under the pretense of creating her carefree image.

I wound my arm around her and pulled her back against my chest as Dexter, one of the guys from the AV club, went on and on about his new drone. He wanted to fly it around the lake and thought it'd be cool to do so while I was rowing my boat through the water, and it wasn't so much that I wasn't interested, as that my attention kept getting drawn back to Kate. I swear, every guy in the near vicinity was suddenly looking at her with interest, and while I promised I wouldn't do anything too possessive, I wanted to claim her as mine, so they'd stop checking her out.

Because she was my friend, and if all these other guys asked her out, she'd be too busy to spend time with me. For the deal we'd made. That was it.

Her intoxicating perfume filled my senses and she wrapped her hand around my arm, holding it against her. Our little performance seemed so innocent when I proposed it; now it was taking on a new life, and my body kept forgetting it was all an act.

I needed to calm down my thoughts, too, or Kate would notice and everyone would see, and this would turn awkward quickly.

"Ugh, when did *that* happen?" The shrill voice caused me to twist my head. Paris, Amber, and the rest of their crew stared at me and Kate, and to say they didn't look happy about how close we were was an understatement.

Kate's attention turned to them, too, the easygoing vibe I'd finally helped her reach fading.

Why do they care? Paris and I shared a physics class together, and admittedly, things had been on the flirty side all semester, but besides one party two months ago where we kissed a little, nothing else happened. She was too shallow for anything long-term, the kind of girl who bounced from guy to guy as the wind changed. I used to be friends with Amber, mostly because our houses were right next to each other, but we hadn't exchanged more than the basic minimum all year. To be fair, she looked more surprised than angry like the rest of them, and part of me thought there might even be a hint of...regret?

Kate spun in my arms, bringing us chest to chest. Well, her chest hit more my upper stomach, something I was going to pretend I didn't notice. I was getting hella good at this whole pretend thing. "I told you she hates me," she said.

"Ignore them." My words didn't calm her like they had when we'd been alone in my truck. I cupped her cheek, forcing her gaze back to mine. "I thought of a punch line." At her confused expression, I added, "To why the chicken crossed the road. Only I'm changing it to why did the chicken*s* cross the road."

"Why?"

"Because they lacked individual thought and all the other chickens were doing it."

The smile came on slowly, but once it took hold, it transformed her features, turning her back into the girl with the contagious smile, who did things like knit beanies, talk to her pet lizard, and ship TV couples with a passion I'd never seen before. "Thanks, wingman."

"Ooh, I love it when you use pet names."

She laughed, and by the time I dared a quick glance at the girl squad who'd obviously hurt her, they'd moved on to judge other people.

I grimaced when I noticed Paris heading for Pecker. She draped herself around him, and considering their history and what I knew about the girl, I suspected she was more his type than Kate.

Kate was way too good for him, obviously, but I knew I'd never convince her of that.

"What?" she asked, and the section of hair that forever fell in her eyes drifted forward. Thanks to earlier tonight, I knew it was as soft as it looked. I wanted to brush it back again, but I needed to limit myself. To not get too carried away with our act, or I might forget where the lines were.

Over her shoulder, I noticed Pecker looked bored by Paris, which I supposed was good for our mission. Was it bad to wish that he'd find a prom date tonight, and then Kate could abandon this plan and not end up hurt?

I swear if he hurts her…

Kate put her hand on the side of my face, the way I'd done to her a moment ago. "Why did the cock cross the road?"

My jaw dropped for a couple of seconds before I recovered. "Why?"

"To grab the chick's ass."

I laughed. "I think you win."

"Well, you looked like you might murder someone. I thought I'd lighten the mood."

"Mood officially lightened." I was about to point out we now had an audience that included her dream boy, but I figured it'd only make her nervous. Which meant limits were off, at least for a couple of seconds. I picked up a strand of her hair, wound it around my finger, and leaned close. I kissed her cheek, just a little peck, and whispered, "Wanna get out of here?"

She licked her lips and I nearly groaned. For a moment the rest of the world faded. But then her eyes flicked to the side. Dawning overcame her features, and she curled my shirt in her fist and tugged me close enough that my nose brushed hers. "Definitely."

I probably should've taken Kate right home—it was almost eleven, after all. But she said she had until eleven thirty, and if I went home and went to bed, then it'd be tomorrow, and I wasn't ready for it to be tomorrow yet.

So we grabbed sodas and walked to the nearest dock. We sat at the end, and Kate's legs went to swinging. "I'm trying to remember for sure which house is yours. I know it's by the dock we usually go to, but there are three, and they all look the same." She squinted. "Doesn't it have green trim? Not that I can even see what color the trim is right now."

"Blue trim." I pointed across the cove. The lights blazed through most of the windows in the house, even though I knew Dad was most likely still in his office, and Mom was up in her room, reading or watching TV alone. "Fifth one down."

Kate counted under her breath until her finger lined up with the right house. "It's nice. With a side of super huge."

"Sometime I'll have to show you the inside." Sometime when Dad wasn't there. Ever since I didn't act excited enough by the internship he'd set up, things were more icy than usual between us. I could only imagine if I told him how I actually felt about it and the entire future he wanted for me.

"I'd like that." The wood creaked underneath us as Kate continued to swing her legs. Must be all that frantic energy buzzing just underneath the surface. Her head tipped to the sky. The moon waned gibbous and put out enough light to cast a pale yellow glow on Kate's features. "Do you still know all the constellations, and, like, the history of all the stars?"

"No."

She whipped her head toward me. "Liar."

"There are billions and billions of stars. You think I know the history of each one?"

"Is it true that most of the stars we see are dead? Because that's depressing, and I like to think they're still up there shining their little butts off."

"Light travels at about 300,000 kilometers a second, which is crazy fast, but stars are so far away that even light from the closest stars takes years to get to us."

She frowned at me. "So you're saying they're dead instead of letting me believe my happier version?"

"I'm giving you facts."

"Fine," she said, her voice making it clear she was all put out about it. "I'll allow it."

"You'll *allow* facts?" Before I got way off topic and fell into a lecture about how facts were facts, even if you didn't want them to be, I shifted back to the subject at hand. "Don't go getting all sad. I wasn't finished. Stars have crazy long lifespans, and depending on size, we're talking high millions to trillions of years. So, no, the answer to your question is that despite popular opinion—which is not the same as proven facts—it's not true. Some of the stars we're seeing might be dead, but most of them—to borrow your phrase—are still shining their little butts off."

"I thought you didn't know their history."

Part of me felt like growling in exasperation, and the other part of me just wanted to throw my arms around her and hug her. All of my perfume sniffing must've killed a few brain cells.

"Glad we cleared that up." She took a swig of her soda and then set the can down on the dock with a *clank*. "Now, tell me the constellations, because I know you know them. Do you still have that app?"

"I have a better one."

"Well, whip it out, Galileo."

"Okay, okay. But you might want to be careful about instructing guys to 'whip it out.' Just saying."

She gasped and shoved me. I chuckled and righted myself, then set my empty soda can next to hers. I opened my stargazer app and lined it up so the constellations would show on the screen.

There were still nights when I laid back and stared up at the stars, but I rarely took the time to study the sky anymore. Considering the calming effect, I should try it out every time my father brought up my summer internship or college. I'd also expressed an interest in marine biology last year, and he'd told me that my head was always in the stars or in the water, and I needed to learn to keep it on solid ground.

Kate leaned in, much closer than she had that summer a few years ago, when she seemed to be doing it more out of polite pity than interest.

I moved the screen into the position that found the most constellations. I pointed out the Big Dipper, which was the one most people knew, then moved on to Virgo and Corona Borealis. "There's Hercules. See?"

The lines on the screen shifted as I honed in on it, outlining the stars.

"And what's the story behind that?" The breeze stirred up the scent of the lake, that fresh-water and pine smell, and it mixed in with Kate's perfume. Suddenly it took a lot more effort than usual to focus on her words instead of the press of her warm body against my arm. "I mean, I know who Hercules is, but why did he get a constellation?"

I thought about feigning ignorance, but this was Kate, and how often did I get to talk about the stars? "As the mother of a dragon, I'm not sure you'll like it too much. He's standing victoriously on Draco's head. Killing the dragon Ladon is thought to be Hercules's biggest victory."

"If Hercules came near my dragon, I'd take him out." She held up her fists as if she were ready for a fight.

"You're just going to take on one of the strongest heroes in mythology?"

"To save Klaus? Um, yeah."

My hand found its way to hers. "I'd put my money on you."

"I might not have had the patience to hear about this a few years ago, but I'm finding it really cool now. So what happens when you point it at someone's face?" She took my phone out of my hands and aimed the screen at me.

"I can't see it," I said, "but I'm guessing nothing happens besides seeing a really dark outline of my face."

"Wrong. I can see this constellation that represents a story about a boy named Cooper, who dreamed about sailing, until one day, his father—Zeus, of course, because Zeus has trouble keeping it in his pants…"

"Maybe someone instructed him to 'whip it out.'"

Kate lowered the screen long enough to give me a

reprimanding look. "*Anyway,* Zeus knew how much his son Cooper loved the sea, so he gave him a magical rowboat that could withstand even the wildest storms, and asked Poseidon to watch out for him." Her eyes peeked over the top of the screen, the phone covering her nose and mouth. "And now he travels the seas, barking orders to go faster, all in pursuit of the most impressive time in the seven seas." She shot me an over-the-top grin.

I took my phone from her and shook my head. "Smart-ass."

"I've exhausted all my Greek mythology knowledge, anyway."

"What? You don't ship any couples from back then?"

"Of course I do." She pulled up one knee and tucked her chin on top of it. "I mean, I'm sure I would if I knew more about them. I'll do some research over the weekend and get back to you on that."

"Can't wait." I made sure it came out on the teasing sounding end of the spectrum, but honestly, it was the truth.

"And if they don't have any constellations for them, we're gonna have to fix that. So you better be prepared, or else."

This time, *I* saluted *her*.

She laughed, the happy sound echoing across the waves, only to come back and smack me right in the chest.

She glanced at the time and sighed. "My mom's cool and all, but I probably shouldn't push it." She jumped to her feet and extended a hand to me, like I'd need help to get up.

I didn't, but I wasn't going to pass up the chance to hold on to her, just for a second or two. *Yep, way too much perfume-sniffing, and I think talking constellations did a number on me, too.*

I stepped on the soda cans, flattening them so I could pack them back easier, because nothing drove me more crazy than people who left their trash everywhere—especially on the shores of my lake.

Kate practically bounced her way down the dock, her excitement for life in general contagious. "I think tonight went pretty well. I actually talked to Mick, like more than a sentence, too, and he knew my name already, which shows promise." Her mouth twisted. "It's a little weird that most of our classmates think we're off hooking up right now, but I guess if it works, it's worth it."

"Totally worth it," I said, with much more conviction than I felt. Then, because I liked it when Kate was happy, I added, "Operation Prom Date is off to a promising start."

Kate held her hand up for a high-five and I slapped my palm to hers. "Hooah!"

Chapter Thirteen

COOPER

When I approached Kate on Monday morning, she had a bigger crowd than usual around her. Well, usually she was alone, so that wasn't very hard. But Jaden, Dexter, and the stoner dude whose name I couldn't recall stood next to her.

She flashed me a big smile and lifted her hand in a wave. "Morning, Cooper."

"Hey, Coop," Jaden said, pushing himself off the locker he was lounging against. "We were just talking about the party. Did you hear the cops broke it up around eleven? Noise complaint, apparently."

"Glad we took off before then." Kate winked at me. I wished I could enjoy it more, but I couldn't help noticing the way the guys in the near vicinity—including my closest friend and usual rowing partner—were looking at her. She had on a black scoop neck top, these tight, bright blue pants, and the silver ribbon she'd tied around her dark hair to form a headband somehow made the look more sexy than innocent.

Like she was a good girl just waiting to go bad.

Damn vultures. They saw a sweet girl with a nice body, and now that they thought she might be open to a little fun, they swooped in to take advantage of that sweetness.

I moved over to her, stepping slightly in front of her. "Yeah. Guess it's good that we took off early."

Kate's hand curled around my arm, and I glanced down, my icy mood thawing a bit.

But she wasn't looking at me. Her teeth sunk into her bottom lip as she grinned at none other than Mick Pecker, that lucky bastard.

"Hey, Kate," he said, a cocky smile on his stupid face. "We still need to have that conversation about colleges."

"Totally." Her voice came out breathless, yet loud enough to make my pulse kick up a notch, and from the goofy look on Pecker's face, he felt the impact, too. She ran her finger across her silver necklace, causing the fat charm there to swing back and forth in a hypnotizing fashion. "Find me later?"

He nodded and moved on, but he cast another glance over his shoulder before he turned the corner.

Great. Suddenly she was all smooth and flirty? What had I done? I was starting to hate myself for thinking this would work—I mean, it *had* worked. So I guess I mostly hated myself for being successful.

"Who knew that one party was all it'd take for my classmates to see me instead of see through me," Kate said, her voice low so that only I'd hear. "Monte's locker is right next to mine, and the only thing he's ever said to me before is 'Please move.'"

Jaden patted the books under his arm. "I better get to class. One more tardy and I have to serve in detention." He looked at me. "You coming, Callihan?"

"One sec." I turned to Kate. "Meet me at my truck after school?"

"That's the plan."

"I just wanted to make sure you weren't going to claim to be too sore so you could try to wiggle out of it."

Her mouth dropped, her expression mock shock. "I wouldn't dream of it. Especially after you delivered so impressively this weekend." She said the last part loud enough it gained the attention of not just the guys who'd already been swarming, but several more people. She probably didn't realize how it sounded, either.

My gaze traveled over her in an attempt to land on somewhere that didn't give me inappropriate thoughts, but every place it landed only made me think about her hips, her butt, her curves, her lips, and that eye-grabbing silver ribbon.

That bow under her ear is just begging for one good yank. I wanted to be the one to do it, too. *And that's definitely my cue to go.*

"I'll catch you later, then." As I started away, I heard someone else call her name.

At least I'd secured every afternoon for the next few weeks before she turned into the most popular girl in school.

I quickened my pace and caught up to Jaden, but I couldn't help casting one more glance Kate's way.

"She's cute," Jaden said.

"I know." *In fact, more and more, it's all I can think about.*

"So you and her are…?"

"Friends."

"Good to know." The smug smile that spread across his face made me want to punch it off him, something I never felt toward Jaden, even when we argued about training and times.

"Don't bother. She's interested in Pecker." As soon as the words were out of my mouth, I realized I shouldn't have said them. She got weird about people knowing, and there were too many ears around. I'd reacted more out of wanting to keep the competition down, even though there was no competition.

She wanted Mick. She had an operation named for landing him and everything. And apparently I needed to be reminded of that fact over and over.

. . .

I thought I looked forward to the end of the school day and getting out on the lake before, but adding Kate to the mix took my anticipation to the next level. At least at the lake, it was just me and her, none of her ever-growing fan club.

Instead of making me maneuver the boat into the water myself on Wednesday afternoon, she took the initiative. But she definitely paused to scan the water, and I immediately knew why.

Yesterday we'd seen Pecker from afar—he was in a kayak and far enough away the only thing Kate could do was wave and yell hello—but it probably gave them something to talk about today, and stupid me, I'd given her that tip. I figured it was the lesser of the evils between rowing over to him and watching them flirt as I sat in the boat like a chump.

Thanks to overhearing a conversation between him and one of his cohorts last period, at least I knew today they were planning on playing football at the school field.

She's all mine today. I shook my head at myself, because that sounded a little too creepy villain for my tastes. What I meant was we wouldn't have any distractions of the jock kind. Not to mention the sun was shining, birds were happily chirping—something Kate had pointed out she loved—and all that glistening water was just begging to be glided across.

Kate gave up her search and focused on the boat. "You want to jump in first?"

"Go ahead. I'll hold it for you."

She shrugged and climbed in. I stepped inside, balancing

my weight to keep the boat from wobbling too much. I sat down and grabbed the oars, ready to get out there, but then I decided we could take a few minutes to catch up—she'd been texting about some group assignment the entire drive over.

"How was your day?" I asked.

She smiled, and that strange sensation I forgot existed until she fully crashed into my life twisted my gut. "Amazing, actually. I talked to Mick before school. We had a whole conversation and everything, about how I saw him on the lake yesterday, and he seemed to be super impressed I came out here all the time. We both talked about how it was one of our favorite places. There might've been an awkward pause or two, but I recovered quickly enough I don't think it was a big deal. Chatting with you all the time has helped me not be so rusty."

The twisty sensation stopped dead in its tracks and tumbled down to my feet. *Go me.*

"He asked for my number, too. Now I just have to hope he uses it, while not staring at my phone, begging for it to ring. I guess that's one point for leaving it in your truck, even if that's mostly so I don't drop it in the water, because that's so something I'd do." She reached down and messed with the strap of her sandal, and I noticed her hot pink toenails matched the neon fingernails I'd focused on entirely too much as she'd texted away in my truck. "But don't worry, I'm not going to sit around and wait, either. By the end of this week, I'm going to deploy some new strategies. I don't have time to go slow. It ups the stakes, but today's the first time I didn't feel completely over my head."

I cleared my throat, but my voice still came out like I'd swallowed sandpaper. "That's great. Pretty soon you won't need me at all."

She lunged across the boat, making it rock, and grabbed my hand. "No way. I'm not ready to go out there without a safety net yet. We still have at least a couple weeks on our deal, right?"

As usual, I couldn't let the girl down, even if this mission was starting to make me less and less happy. The buzz of a challenge wasn't there anymore. In fact, it was the opposite of how challenges tended to go for me, like the more I succeeded, the less the urge to fist pump. But I worked to cover my true feelings, because she'd done her part, and this wasn't about me. "Right. I'm here for you, as long as you need me."

The tension leaked out of her posture. "Good. I'd be totally lost on this stuff without you."

I pulled my hand out of hers before I could think about how good it felt in mine—okay, so maybe I was too late, but at least I tried. "We better get training. Are you still sore?"

"Nope. I'm always exhausted by the end, but the soreness is finally gone. Plus, I've got all these happy vibes traveling through me from today's success, so I feel like I could go forever."

I gripped the edge of my seat, the sensation in my gut going from beat-up attraction to biting jealousy. *This is why I wasn't supposed to get so involved. I don't have much free time left, and we'll all just be going to college in a few months anyway, and none of this stuff will matter.*

Kate took hold of her oars. "What's your fastest time with Jaden? Because I'm ready to take it down."

"It's going to take a lot more than not being sore." As soon as the words were out of my mouth, regret rushed up. Her crestfallen expression gave it sharp claws that made the regret dig deeper and make a home in my chest.

Since I didn't know what to say—and it's not like I could explain I was only frustrated my help with landing her dream date was being so effective—I spun around in my seat and took hold of my oars. I twisted my wrist so I could see my watch. "Ready?"

"Ready," she said, much less enthusiastic than she'd been moments ago.

Then we were off, oars gliding through the water, sights set on the other side.

Chapter Fourteen

Kate

Excitement had zipped through me all day, keeping me on a constant high.

Until I'd gotten into the boat with Coach Grouchy Pants. Stupid me, I'd been anticipating the moment we'd be alone on the water again. We had such a great weekend together, and the past few days I thought we'd really connected. That we understood each other in that sort of way two people did where they could communicate without words. Although, for the record, I liked communicating with words. Lots of them, often all strung together. The silence hanging in the air made me antsy, and I instinctively wanted to fill it with anything and everything. But Cooper didn't deserve my chatter.

Klaus is going to get an earful when I get home, so I hope he's had his twenty hours of sleep already.

Two ducks flew overhead and landed in the water a few feet away.

They immediately swam over and quacked at each other,

as if they were checking in on the other's landing. *Aww*.

"Kate! Are you paying attention? You're getting off pace!"

I whipped my head forward to see Cooper looking at me over his shoulder, and my irritation must've shown through, because his eyes widened, like he knew he was about to get it.

I dropped my oars. "For your information, I'm *not* paying attention to your stupid pace. I'm watching two ducks. They're cute and they're nice to each other, and right now, I'm about to jump in the water and go hang out with *them* instead of you."

Cooper pressed his lips together, and at first I thought it was fear, but then he seemed to be fighting laughter.

"No, you don't get to laugh." I stood. "I know I sometimes jokingly refer to you as Coach Grouchy Pants, but today you're taking it to the next level. You're Coach Jerk Face."

Sputtered laughter came out, and when I scowled at him, he slowly stood and turned to face me, his hands up in surrender. "You're right. I've been a jerk face today."

I crossed my arms. "You'll get no argument from me."

He took a step and the boat wobbled. "I'm sorry. I was in a bad mood."

"Well, don't take it out on me."

Cooper glanced at the ducks. "Do you ship them?"

"Not that I have to, because they're clearly already in love, but yes. I hope they have a very happy duck life and have lots of beautiful duck children."

"I think the word you're searching for is ducklings, because children are a human thing. Duck children sounds like a mutant science experiment gone wrong."

"Ugh, you drive me crazy!" I shoved him, and he barely caught his balance.

"I just thought a math girl would be more into facts, is all."

I moved to shove him again, and he caught my arm. The boat rocked, and I fell into Cooper, my hands braced against his chest. Despite trying not to think about it, my hands noticed how firm it was. I also caught a whiff of woodsy cologne, and there was something intoxicating about the way it mixed in with the fresh air and water scent.

"Careful," Cooper warned, his deep voice vibrating against my palms. "You're about to send us both into the water."

"I don't want to be careful." I straightened. "I love the lake, and I want to enjoy my time out here. I'm glad you love rowing and all, but sometimes you've got to slow down for a moment and appreciate it." I squatted next to the side, curving my hands around the edge of the wooden boat, and peered into the water. Underneath the surface, a couple of fish darted back and forth. "There's an entire life under there and you're missing it."

Cooper knelt next to me, his thigh pressed against mine, and warmth wound through me. "I get what you're saying," he said. "No more being so serious."

"Seriously." In one fluid motion, I scooped up a handful of water and launched it at him.

His jaw dropped. He blinked at me through wet lashes, and then he lunged. With a squeal, I scrambled backward, attempting to flee—I'm not sure where, but I suppose there was something to be said for trying.

Unfortunately Cooper was too fast. He launched a spray of water at me and all I could do was throw my hands in front of me to try to block another attack. The boat rocked as I attempted to stand, and I flung out my arms, trying to brace myself on something.

Strong hands caught me around the waist. I gripped Cooper's wrists, clinging on for dear life. The rocking of the boat calmed, but I couldn't say the same for my heart rate.

Instead of coming back down, it tripped over its beats, each one faster than the next.

The weirdo attraction vibes caught me off guard and overwhelmed me, so I did the only thing I could think of. I rocked the boat again, trying to get the teasing vibe back. Only I overdid it, my attempt to turn the tides apparently endowing me with super strength.

I bumped into him, and he tipped, his hands flailing now. "I'm sorry, I—"

He reached out and caught hold of my wrist, and then we both went tumbling over the side, into the icy cold water.

Chapter Fifteen

I broke the surface with a gasp, the jolt from the cold water like a hundred volts of electricity being fired into my body.

Kate bobbed up a second later. "Oh my gosh, it's cold!"

"Hey, you're the one who decided to throw me into the water."

A shiver wracked her body. "I meant to make you almost fall, not actually fall. And I like how you took me with you."

"I just figured you'd want to follow your own advice about enjoying the water."

She splashed water at me. "Oh, sure. *Now* you listen to me."

I slapped the surface of the water with my palm out, sending a spray at her. We laughed, and then we fired at will, stream after stream. Some crashed in the middle, and some hit their target.

Little by little, my body got used to the cold water. Or maybe it grew numb, but either way, it wasn't so bad anymore.

Kate ran her hands through her hair, slicking it back away from her face. "Okay, let's see who can spin all the way around and come back up faster. Ready...? Go!"

I dove under the surface, tucking and spinning, and kicked for all I was worth.

She was already up and waiting. "You lose." She added a victory dance, doing some kind of chicken thing with her arms as she made an *oot-oot* taunting noise.

"And you wonder why I get so serious about winning. Where's my 'good try; you'll get 'em next time'?"

"Good try, sport, but you had your ass handed to you." She giggled, apparently thinking she was hilarious. And okay, she kinda was.

"Fine. Let's see who can hold their breath longer." I lifted my fingers toward my nose to plug it.

"No way." Kate shook her head. "In, like, every movie where they do that, the other dude doesn't come up, and then the person is left swimming alone, calling their name in a panic."

"You've seen too many movies," I said.

"Go ahead and hold your breath, then. If the sea monster gets you while you're down there, just know that I'm not coming after you."

I laughed and swam closer. I reached down and grabbed her leg, laughing harder when she squealed. She kicked me and stuck out her tongue. "Jerk."

Unlike when she called me Coach Jerk Face earlier, this time there was a lighter, joking tone to her voice.

Suddenly she lurched toward me, her arms wrapping around my neck. "Okay, for reals, I just felt something slip past my leg." Her gaze skimmed the surface of the lake. "I'm telling myself it's just a fish, but it felt like a really big fish."

"There are some pretty big fish in here." I paused for dramatic effect. "Then there's the alligators."

"I know there aren't any alligators," she said with a click of her tongue, but she still searched the area around us.

"Okay, but I know for a fact that the police caught a couple last year." It was true, but they were little ones, and the police concluded they were pets someone had abandoned. If the owners had done any research, they'd know the water was way too cold in the winter for alligators to survive it. But I wasn't going to tell Kate that quite yet—messing with her was too much fun. "Do you see the way the water's parting over there? I thought it was a log, but a log doesn't move like that."

She practically crawled up me, her grip on my neck nearing chokehold levels. "Not funny."

I was going to tease her some more, because we hadn't even covered snake territory yet, but then I noticed the soft press of her curves, and how if I looked down, I could see her skin and her polka dot bra through her shirt. And then I couldn't stop looking and noticing, even though I knew I shouldn't be.

My breath grew shallow, and for a couple of seconds, I forgot I needed to continue to tread water, and we started dipping lower.

"Okay, I think that's enough enjoying the lake by being inside of it today. I'm ready to get back to rowing." Kate let go of me and swam toward the boat, and as she climbed in, I noticed a few other things I shouldn't. Namely her legs and the way her clothes molded to her body, every curve on display.

Get it together, Callihan. Still, I couldn't help thinking she was right earlier when she said I didn't slow down enough to enjoy the actual lake. I was in such a hurry to be on the water as much as possible before my time ran out that I forgot to actually appreciate the ability to get lost out here. The sense of calm it brought to my life, and how it felt more like my home than my house sometimes.

I lifted myself into the boat and returned Kate's smile.

Goose bumps covered her skin and water dripped from her hair and clothes into a puddle on the boat floor. The bit of makeup she'd had on was long gone, and the last rays of the sun spotlighted her natural beauty and those features I was starting to crave seeing.

Kate wadded her hair in her hands and wrung it out. "Did you want to tell me how I was right about how fun it can be to slow down once in a while now, or later?"

I could think of so many girls who would've yelled at me for pulling them into the water fully clothed, and how there'd be talk about ruined clothes and hair and makeup. Kate had to be freezing, but she was sitting there all smug, grinning like she'd just had the best adventure.

While I was slowing down and enjoying things, I figured I should add the time she and I had left together to that list, too.

By the time we made it back to my truck, we were both cold and tired. Kate was still in a happy mood, but I worried she'd catch pneumonia or something, like every person over the age of forty threatened kids they'd do if they didn't cart around big coats 24/7.

I cranked the heater and looked behind my seat. "Jackpot." I handed my hoodie over to Kate.

"But what about you?"

"I'm fine," I said, ignoring the squish of my jeans against the seat as I moved to start the truck. "Just put it on. Please."

She nodded and tugged it over her head. Unfortunately, with her wet clothes, I knew she'd still be far from warm. The twenty-minute drive to her house didn't usually seem like a big deal, but that long being cold and wet—not to mention all the time we'd spent on the lake that way—was adding up fast.

My house sat behind us, a dim outline against the setting

sun.

Wednesday meant Dad played golf this afternoon, and he almost always went drinking with the good old boys after. Since his current case left his stress level high, things were tenser at home between him and Mom as well right now, so most likely he'd stay out late.

"This is crazy riding around in wet clothes like this," I said. "Why don't we go dry off and warm up at my place, and then I'll drive you home later?"

Kate hugged her arms around herself as she cast a quick glance at my house. She nodded, her teeth chattering together. "Okay. I'll just text my mom and let her know."

Her eyes widened when she took her phone out of my glove box. "Mick texted me. He actually texted me! I figured it was a long shot, or that he'd take days, but"—her voice pitched higher—"he texted me!"

She tapped on the screen and her happy expression morphed into one of confusion.

Was it wrong to hope he'd said something extremely stupid or jackass-ish? Something that would land him way past the ten spot on her Kanye Douchebag Scale, so he'd look a lot worse than me.

"All it says is 'what's up?'" She turned the screen to me and practically shoved it in my face, so close the words blurred. "What am I supposed to do with this?"

Ignore him and keep hanging out with me. For no other reason than to have fun. Needing a distraction, I drove the few yards to park in my driveway. Of course when I stopped the truck she was still looking at me all expectantly. "Uh, type: just messing around with Cooper at the lake."

"Yeah, but if he thinks I'm with you all the time, won't he start thinking I'm with you, *with you* and stop talking to me?"

One can only hope. I knew that my hope was in vain, though, because that'd require him being a gentleman, and he wasn't much of one. So he'd read between the lines and take it as she and I were messing around, and turn it into how he wanted to mess around with her, which sent enough heat through my veins that I wasn't all that cold anymore. *It's what she wants. Why she's here with you in the first place.*

I tried to remind myself *yet again* that I was avoiding drama and getting carried away with Kate and the *act* we put on in public for her mission, and forced my reply through clenched teeth. "Trust me. Send the text."

She spoke the words as she typed, the exact ones I'd fed to her, and then she sent the text about going to my house to her mom.

I wasn't nearly as eager to take her inside after that stupid texting thing, but it didn't change the fact that she needed warm, dry clothes. I called out for my mom as I ushered Kate inside, but she didn't answer, so it looked like we had the place to ourselves.

I took her up to my room and dug through my drawers until I found a T-shirt and some sweats I'd outgrown years ago. I pointed her toward the bathroom adjacent to the guestroom so she could take a hot shower and get her body temperature up.

I broke off to my bathroom to do the same, and about fifteen minutes later, we met back up in the hallway. I took her wet clothes and tossed them into the dryer, trying not to let my eyes linger when I spotted the polka dot bra among her things. It had a pink bow in the middle.

Okay, so I failed at not lingering.

When I returned to my room, Kate was seated on my desk chair, twisting it one way and then the other. My too-long sweat pants pooled around her ankles and she had the sleeves of my hoodie rolled up. Her wet hair looked darker than usual, and it was messy, like she'd tried to finger-comb it, only to abandon the attempt halfway through.

I drank in the view, surprised by how much I enjoyed seeing her in my clothes, in my room, and a word that had no business being there popped into my head: *mine*.

But then my gaze lifted to her face.

She had on that fixated, calculating expression that instinctively sent trepidation through my gut. Those big green eyes came back from whatever planet they'd been visiting and focused on me. Something told me I wasn't going to like the next words out of her mouth. "Mick didn't text me back yet."

Guess I was wrong. That's not so ba—

"I assume you have a laptop somewhere around here? Can you pull up his social media profiles and help me do some light recon?"

And there it is.

"Hear me out," she said, rolling the chair toward me. "Remember there's a tight deadline."

As if I could forget.

"And I just feel like I'm not utilizing every tool at my disposal, and clearly I need all the help I can get. With your input to guide me, surely I can figure out what I need to do to get to the next level. Plus, when I'm on my profile, I'm always worried I'll accidentally hit Like on an old picture and look like a total stalker."

Yeah, we wouldn't want it to look like that.

"Not that I look all the time. Only once in a while, really." One more scoot brought her knees to mine. She reached up and grabbed my hand. "Please."

Two minutes later, we were seated on my bed with my laptop. I scrolled through my Facebook feed.

"You just passed a post that you need to go back to," Kate said. "Quick. Go back, go back!"

I dragged my fingers on the scroll pad until she said, "There."

A picture of a puppy and a kitten snuggling filled the

screen. The post insisted that if you liked it, the world would magically be better to animals, and butterflies and rainbows would rain down amazing karma on you or some shit, but if you ignored it, you'd have bad karma for a year.

I glanced from it to Kate, then slowly scrolled past it again.

Kate *tsked* and shook her head. "So you're saying you don't need any good karma, not for animals and not for you? Even though you have a race coming up?"

"It's more that I don't negotiate with meme terrorists."

Kate tried to hide her laugh. No doubt she liked every damn one of those posts, and because I'd clearly lost my mind over the girl, I found it incredibly endearing. If I had any good karma to give, it was hers.

"Looks like he posted something about an hour ago," Kate said, reaching right over me and clicking over to Mick's profile.

His pictures and deep thoughts filled the screen—I'd really been trying to avoid this. It was why I hadn't just clicked on his profile from the beginning.

"Okay, now you take the wheel," she said. "It makes me too nervous."

I slowly dragged the cursor down, hoping she'd get whatever fix she was looking for and the torture would end soon.

Kate's fingers brushed my knee. "Wait, scroll up again."

My pulse quickened as she rested her hand where her fingers had brushed, her touch soaking through the thin cotton of my sweats. I swallowed and kept my eyes glued to the screen as I followed her instructions. If I looked at her, I was afraid I'd lose it and either tell her this was ridiculous and I wanted out—in words that'd probably come out way too harsh sounding—or that I'd try to kiss her.

So I just scrolled back up to post 307 of Mick talking about how awesomesauce he was at football and how hard it was for him to choose a school, and in #firstworldproblems news, the coaches from the colleges were calling him every day now.

Woe is you, dude, at least you get a choice. Harvard was nothing to turn my nose up at, and the truth was, I *did* want to go there. They had a great rowing team, and they were number one in marine biology, a subject I'd love to explore more and possibly major in. To go and study political science instead? It seemed like a wasted opportunity. But I didn't dare say that to dear old Dad.

Kate made a *hmmm* noise. "Okay, go to his recent check-ins…"

I stop and say hi to a girl I kinda sorta know one day after school, and now it's come to this… Cyber stalking a guy I can't stand for someone I want to stand close to a little more than I should.

She leaned close enough I could feel the warmth radiating off her body. *Okay, a* lot *more than I should.*

Chapter Sixteen

My phone chimed and I nearly jumped out of Cooper's too big clothes. "It's him," I whispered when a text from Mick flashed across the screen. "Quick, close that down."

"Gladly," Cooper said, slamming his laptop shut. "For the record, he can't see you through the phone."

"I feel like he'll sense it."

Cooper gave me a *you're insane* look that would've been easier to dispute *before* he'd seen how well I knew how to maneuver around Mick's Facebook page.

Better keep the other places I use for recon to myself. Everyone knew that thanks to the adults on there, Facebook was where you censored yourself more anyway.

With the computer now closed and put away on the nightstand, I opened the text.

Future Prom Date: *Are you and Callihan a thing?*

"Future Prom Date?" Cooper's scowl made his dimples

disappear for a moment. "How'd I miss that the first time you shoved your phone in my face?"

"I was going for resolute," I said, curling my phone closer. "It seemed like a good way to help my goals come true. Like all that visualization crap athletes talk about before a big game. Don't you do it for rowing?"

"No."

"I don't believe you."

Cooper let out a long breath. "Okay, so maybe our coach has talked about it. But if someone sees that on your phone—especially Pecker—he'll freak." His eyebrows arched up and he put a hand on his chest. "That's why you recruited me. To tell you that kind of thing before it blows up in your face."

"Noted." I lifted my phone and ran my thumb across the glass, getting a residual thrill over Mick texting me in the first place. "What do I say to him? I mean, clearly, I say no, we're not a thing. Right?"

"Wrong." Cooper shifted, the navy and white comforter bunching underneath him. "You dodge. Make him guess. Here—" He snatched my phone from me.

"Hey! Have I ever told you that you have boundary issues?"

"You're in *my* room, wearing *my* clothes, making me stalk a guy on *my* laptop. Let's not get into boundary issues."

He had a point there. His bedroom was nice, too—spacious and cleaner than I expected, and before he'd come in, I'd checked out the killer view of the lake from his huge windows. And speaking of his clothes, they were soft and warm and smelled faintly like him. I was considering crossing a big boundary and claiming his hoodie as my own so I'd never have to take it off, and it had to do more with wanting to hold on to the sense of security I felt than simply being warm.

The *tap, tap* of my phone's keyboard brought me back to

the current situation, and I scooted closer and watched him type out a response, hypnotized by his long fingers and the way the line in his forearm twitched as he typed.

Until I read the words.

Me (well, Cooper posing as me): *We hang out sometimes. Did you text me to talk about him, or do you want to know what I'm doing this weekend?*

I gasped and reached for the phone, my chest meeting the hard resistance of his shoulder. "You can't send that!"

Cooper held it out of my reach and hit send. "Too late. You can thank me later."

"You know, I felt bad about dunking you in the water today, but now I'm glad. If I were you, I'd sleep with one eye open." I lunged for my phone again and Cooper and I fell off the foot of the bed, ending up in a tangle of limbs on the floor.

Cooper groaned. "Hanging out with you is hazardous to my health."

I got the giggles as I tried to untangle myself from him, but he shifted forward as I reached across him for my phone, and I ended up in his lap, our noses all but touching.

The mood shifted, the air heavy and thick, and I sat frozen, transfixed by his eyes and the way they locked on to mine. Our dip in the lake had left the waves in his hair more defined, bordering on curly territory, and before I realized what I was doing, I reached up and pulled on the lock that hung down on his forehead.

His breath stuttered, and mine didn't feel so steady, either. I licked my lips, and he made a low noise in the back of his throat. Awareness zinged through me as my heart beat a rapid rhythm against my rib cage.

A loud throat clearing broke the silence, and I looked toward the doorway, where a blond woman stood.

I scrambled to my feet and Cooper did the same. "Hey,

Mom. This…isn't what it looks like." He tugged on his shirt. "I know that's what every kid says when he gets caught doing something against the rules, but we fell into the lake, and Kate was soaking wet, so that's why she's wearing my clothes, and—"

The woman held up a hand. "It's okay. You're lucky I wasn't your dad."

Cooper nodded.

"All the same, why don't you and…Kate, was it?"

I swallowed, but my voice still came out squeaky. "Yeah. Um, nice to meet you?"

A small smile curved her lips. "You, too. Now, why don't you come down to the kitchen and I'll make some dinner."

"You're going to cook?" Cooper asked, and the woman gave him a look. There was a bit of reprimanding in the mix, but there was softness and affection, too.

"I can make grilled cheese, as you well know," she said.

"Right. And cereal."

She laughed, and I hoped that meant we weren't going to get into huge trouble. I could handle, like, a tiny bit of trouble, but if anyone yelled, I cracked and panicked.

Cooper picked up my phone and gave it to me. For some reason, his bringing up how we'd been soaking wet earlier made me recall the way his clothes had clung to his torso, and I got caught up staring at it now. Wet or dry, he knew how to fill out a T-shirt, that was for sure.

"Kate?" Cooper extended his hand. "You coming?"

Part of me was dying to see if Mick had texted back, but there were too many eyes on me right now, and I couldn't refuse Cooper's hand.

Once I took it, warmth tingled through me, pushing all thoughts of checking my phone to the far corner of my mind.

Chapter Seventeen

KATE

As I walked toward the school on Thursday morning, my thoughts were caught up in reliving moments from last night. I'd had such a fun evening with Cooper, from our impromptu swim in the lake to hanging out in his room, and even after that, having dinner with him and his mom.

She was beautiful, the kind of woman I imagined won crowns in pageants. Which was probably why I'd expected her to be cold. Now I mentally kicked myself for stereotyping. I wanted to defend myself by saying I'd been burned by girls who looked like her before, but that was no excuse.

Mrs. Callihan made us grilled cheese, and then I pressed for stories about Cooper—it was only fair that I gather intel on some of his embarrassing moments since he'd witnessed way too many of mine.

"When he was little," Mrs. Callihan had said with a smile, happy to indulge me, "he was obsessed with space, and used to constantly spout off facts about solar systems and planets.

I'd ask him to take out the trash in the evening and then I'd find the trash on the back doorstep, and he'd be out on the shore of the lake with a telescope. I used to call him my little space case." She'd ruffled his hair and he dodged away, his entire face red.

"Thanks, Mom. That's enough stories for now." Cooper had put his hand on my shoulder. "I should probably take Kate home before her mom starts to worry."

"No, no. It's still early." Mrs. Callihan had glanced at the time, and her warm smile faded. "Oh. It's later than I thought." A strange look passed between them, an unspoken conversation I didn't have the translator for.

Since my clothes had dried, I'd changed and Cooper took me home. We hadn't talked much on the way, but it was a comfortable silence, one I hadn't scrambled to try to fill. And not because he didn't deserve my chatter that time.

Bonus, when I'd started to take off his hoodie in the truck, he'd told me to hang on to it so I wouldn't have to be cold for the few steps it took to get to my front door. I'd wanted to wear it to school this morning, but I figured that'd make it look like we were a couple, and our act was supposed to be more casual friends who might be hooking up.

I paused and let that sink in. Honestly, I'd been so wrapped up in how much fun I'd had yesterday evening, I'd almost forgotten that our hangouts were part of a deal. I needed to remember that before I got carried away and started making the confusing tingly attraction vibes I occasionally felt with him into something they weren't.

But we're real friends now, right? Having someone to confide in, someone who made me laugh and even look forward to school had made this last week and a half so much better, and I didn't want to do anything to mess that up.

Which meant chalking up that moment on the floor of his bedroom to not ever being that smooshed up against a boy before and refocusing on my mission. The one he was assisting me with.

Unable to help myself, I took a tiny whiff of the hoodie before placing it in my locker. Just because Cooper had really amazing smelling cologne, and it was okay to think friends smelled sexy.

I grabbed my books for my first class and turned down the hall. I spotted Cooper in the crowd and waved.

He nodded back at me, a grin spreading across his face, and anticipation tingled through my veins.

I started toward him, planning on greeting him by calling him Space Case. But then Mick stepped up to me, and I nearly tripped over my feet. I opened my mouth to speak before realizing I didn't know what to say, and panic rose up.

My teeth popped as I snapped my mouth closed, embarrassingly loud, and my body heated, giving my deodorant a run for its money.

"You never texted me back, you naughty vixen," Mick said.

Oh, how embarrassing. He's not even talking to me. I spun around to see who the lucky girl was, but no one else was around. Which just left me as the recipient of his words, but the thought of me as a naughty vixen was laughable.

My focus got lost in his perfect features, the sharp line of his jaw and that sexy indention in his chin, and the cheekbones that should be illegal on males so that women could have *something* to hold over guys like him.

"Kate?"

I ran a hand through my hair. "It was just so late when I got home, and I didn't want to wake you up."

He nudged me with his elbow, the smirk that frequented my dreams twisting his mouth. "You can wake me up anytime."

Since the open mouth, gasping-for-air fish face couldn't possibly be sexy, I pressed my lips together and forced them into a smile. *I can do this. Carefree, light…*

"I'll make a note." Wait. Note making was serious. "Or I won't."

His eyebrows drew together and nervousness bound my lungs, and talking whilst unable to breathe wasn't as easy as it sounded, and it didn't sound all that easy in the first place.

I reached up and twisted a strand of my hair around my finger. "What I'm saying is, I'll take you up on that sometime."

"Good. So how much longer are you going to leave me hanging about this weekend?"

Crap. He must've said something in the text about this weekend. As soon as I'd walked in the door last night, Mom had wanted all the details, and I'd had to sort through which ones I wanted to give her, and by the time I looked at my phone, it'd died. I was running late this morning, so I hadn't even checked it yet. Which was so unlike me, to the point I wondered if a parasite had been in the lake water and infected my brain.

It certainly wasn't because I'd completely spaced Mick's text and gotten caught up in thinking about my *friend* Cooper and how much fun we had together.

If I dug out my phone now, he might see his code name that I hadn't had time to change. "I'm sorry, but I just realized I have to get notes for this test I'm probably about to fail." *Which is something a serious girl would worry about.* "Not that I'd normally care, but my mom is riding me about my grades, and you know how it is."

Please know how it is, even though I *don't even know how it is.*

"For sure. Coach was always riding my ass about grades — but now that season's over and I've got scholarships lined up, I'm pretty much coasting." He made a motion with his hand, like it was surfing an air-wave.

"Okay, well. I'll catch up with you later? Like lunch?"

Realizing he probably had standing appointments with all the cool kids at lunch, I backtracked. "Or not lunch, because I'm sure you have plans, but—"

He put his hand on my arm and my heart stopped, I swear it did. "I'll catch you at lunch."

With one last smirk, he backed away and melted into the crowd.

As soon as I was sure the target had left the area, I ducked into a corner and pulled out my phone. My fingers hit too many keys at once, and I ended up having to put my password in three times.

Future Prom Date: *I'm having a group of people over on Friday night. How about you be one of them?"*

I squealed loud enough to garner a few stares, then I quickly put my phone away. *Guess I owe Cooper an apology, or thanks, or maybe even dinner.*

I couldn't believe that ballsy text had worked. Clearly I didn't know what guys were looking for in girls, so thank goodness I had help. I scanned the halls for Cooper so I could tell him his plan actually worked, but most everyone was rushing around, headed to class, and I realized I better, too. Didn't want to get my first tardy.

Making it through morning classes had never been so hard. Before lunch I popped a breath mint, slicked on some of my strawberry shimmery lip-gloss, and searched for Mick among the crowd in the cafeteria, feigning ignorance to where he usually sat.

"Kate!" Mick patted the seat next to him, and I had a crap-ton of eyes on me. The sets belonging to the female portion of the crowd were less than friendly.

My heart traveled up into my throat and I carefully put one foot in front of the other, terrified I'd trip and ruin a moment I'd dreamed about for longer than I cared to admit.

As soon as I sat down, Mick put his hand high on my thigh, like we'd been dating for months instead of seconds.

Not that we were, you know, technically dating.

But did he really think he could just put his hand so high on my thigh? Offense bubbled up, because I wasn't that kind of girl, but then I remembered the endgame of this whole operation meant pretending I might be.

Just until I hook him. Then he'll get to know the real me, and I can slowly clue him in to the fact that I move a little slower.

"We never did have that conversation about UNH," I tried, my voice coming out less steady than I hoped, but not as shaky as I feared it would.

"Right." He shifted to face me more fully, keeping his voice low enough to make it a two-person conversation despite the large group surrounding us. "I like that it's only a forty- to fifty-minute drive. I'd still live on campus to keep up with practices, but I'd be close enough to come home when I need to."

Before I could tell him I was planning to stick close, mostly because it was cheaper to live at home, he added, "I'm not one of those people afraid to leave home or anything. It's just…my little brother will be a freshman next year, and he plays football, too. I'd like to be able to at least see some of his games."

Aww. I thought about that day in the ice cream shop again, and how I could see how much his little brother adored him, and clearly it went both ways. "That's sweet."

"Sweet." He rubbed the back of his neck. "I'm not sure how I feel about being called sweet."

"It's a compliment, I promise." I glanced at my food, but knew I'd never be able to eat while he was looking at me so closely. "And UNH is a really good school. I'm actually planning on going to the branch in Manchester." My major was still up in the air, but I was leaning toward statistics. There was a big need for it in the health field and software field, so I had a few career paths to play with.

"It is a good school," Mick said, but something about his posture screamed hesitance.

"So, what's the hang up?"

He arched his eyebrows like I'd surprised him, and maybe I was reading more into the situation, but he seemed relieved I'd noticed. "It's not even in the top one hundred as far as football goes. Which probably makes me sound like a total snob, but I want to play for a good school, one who wins."

"Who doesn't?"

"Exactly. Penn State is top ten. It'll be more competitive, so I might not play as much, but it'd be more recognition. It's just farther away—like, seven hours."

"Hmm. I'm sure your brother will understand that playing college ball will keep you busy. And you could probably sneak in a few games still. There are these things called airplanes that get people places super fast these days."

A big grin broke out across his face and butterflies went to fluttering like crazy in my gut. "Thanks, Kate," he added, and the way he said my name sent those butterflies crashing into each other.

I glanced up to find Paris and her gang glaring at me. Except for Amber—instead of pretending I didn't exist anymore, she gave me a small smile.

I was in the middle of trying to decide if I should return it or attempt a polite hello, or if this was simply some kind of mean-girl trap when Mick shifted even closer. "So?" He moved his lips next to my ear. "About this weekend? You down?"

I twisted to face him and his nose brushed my cheek. My nerve-endings went crazy, a mix of euphoria and weirdness, and I couldn't really pick one emotion out from the other. At least I knew the answer to his question, though.

I slowly licked my lips and then gave him my best flirty smile. "I'm down."

Chapter Eighteen

COOPER

"Did that sandwich sleep with your girlfriend or something?" Jaden asked, drawing my attention back to him. He jerked his chin toward it. "Or are you just planning on mangling it into submission before you take a bite?"

I looked down at the ham and cheese sub that now looked like a barbell, the middle flattened to a skinny handle while the ends bulged out on either side of my fist. My gaze accidentally drifted back to Kate. Kate, who was sitting so close to Pecker that there couldn't be enough oxygen for the both of them in that bubble.

No, my sandwich didn't sleep with my girlfriend, but some jackass had his hands on my girl. Er, my girl friend—friend who was a girl. I wanted to go over and pry his hands off her, but I was the idiot who'd put them there. Apparently my text yesterday had worked.

Again, go me.

If I watched the snuggle fest any more I'd lose my

breakfast, so I forced my focus back to my lunch.

Jaden glanced from their group to me. He opened his mouth and I put up a stop-right-there hand.

"Don't say it. She's just a sweet girl, and I'm afraid he'll hurt her. That's all."

"Whatever you say, man."

Great. Now I was acting like some kind of caveman. I'd never experienced jealousy like this before. The closest I'd come was when I heard someone got a choice in career, or when another team beat ours at one of the regattas, but even that had nothing on this toxic burning sensation eating away at my gut.

Last night I'd let Kate in—into my house, into meeting my mom, who of course told her embarrassing childhood tales. I liked to keep all the parts of my life separate. Made things less complicated.

If she'd merely come over, I could deal. But it was that moment after we'd tumbled off my bed, onto the floor of my room that haunted me. That jolt of electricity, that crackling connection in the air I couldn't have imagined.

If only I'd stuck to keeping my life in those separate boxes.

While I was wishing for things, I also wished my mom had come home about ten minutes later so I'd know if anything would've happened if Kate and I had a little more time alone. Or that Mom would've shown up sooner, so I didn't know what it felt like to have Kate in my arms, her body pressed against mine.

My sandwich seemed to be taking the abuse pretty well, so I shoved it in my mouth a couple giant bites at a time. Then I eyed Jaden, struggling with his spoon.

"I was going to ask if you thought you could row, but it looks like you can't even eat."

"If I could flip you off, I'd do that. Oh, wait, I have another hand." He held up his middle finger.

Despite my sour mood, I laughed.

"Ooh, I'm so gonna tell that you're making crude gestures at school." Alana sat next to her brother and stole one of his potato chips.

Jaden smacked her hand away. "Go hang out with your own friends. Oh, that's right, you only care about grades."

She frowned and shoved his injured arm, clearly not caring about the injured part. "I do not. My boyfriend's just not here today."

"Yeah, I really don't want to hear about your boring boyfriend."

"Because you don't have a girlfriend? Now who's got the lame social life?"

They always went back and forth like this, which I assumed was a sibling thing. The twins thing probably made it even stronger, although giving each other a hard time and their similar complexion and hair color was about all they had in common. Jaden rarely took things very seriously, and Alana made Kate's serious nature seem mild. She was forever talking about earning scholarships, saving money, and being at the top of her classes. She and the junior class president had been dating forever, but all I ever saw them do was study together.

"Do you have a couple dollars?" she asked Jaden. "I need to hit the vending machine."

"Sorry. I don't have any cash. Not that I'd give it to you if I did."

Before another argument broke out, I pulled out my wallet and handed her a five.

"Thanks, Coop. You're the best." She gave me a quick hug. She was the closest thing to a sibling I had, and as she walked toward the vending machine, I noticed she seemed weighed down, like she'd given up faking being okay. I made a note to double-check that that boyfriend of hers was treating her right.

Jaden lifted his splinted arm and turned his elbow. "The wrist doesn't even hurt much anymore; I'm just wearing the splint because of doctor's orders. But by the end of this week, I'm going to ditch it, and another week of icing and rest, and I should be back to my old self. I miss being out on the water."

I missed our impressive times, and he was easy enough to talk to, but I couldn't say I was in a huge hurry to exchange my current partner for him—he just wasn't as nice to look at.

Jaden renewed his struggle with eating with his left hand. "How about today I come help your girl out in the boat? I could at least do that much."

My eyes automatically searched her out, because they didn't learn from their mistakes. Another surge of jealousy pumped through my veins. If Kate thought I was grouchy yesterday, my irritation level had jumped at least three levels from seeing her with him. I didn't want to yell at her, or for her to end up deciding we couldn't even be friends. Regardless of how things turned out with her and Pecker, I didn't want to lose having her in my life during my last few months of freedom.

If having Jaden there to act as a filter until I could get my frustration under control would help maintain that friendship, I'd make it work. Even if it would throw off the weight and strokes. As a bonus, I bet she wouldn't talk about Pecker in front of Jaden. "Meet me at my truck after school." I stood, more than ready to get out of here. "And bring your game face."

• • •

When I accepted Jaden's offer—rather proud of my mad coping skills—I'd neglected to play the scenario all the way out. As in, I failed to factor in that with Jaden in the truck,

Kate would have to sit in the middle, which meant the side of her body pressed against mine, and I couldn't escape the scent of her perfume.

Both windows were cracked, the wind swirling her hair around her face and occasionally into mine.

Finally, I rolled mine up. When I returned my left hand to the steering wheel and put my other one back down, it landed right on her thigh. I picked it up like I'd been burned.

"You okay?" She had that shimmery lip-gloss on her lips and one strand of her hair stuck in it. She reached up, swiping at all the wrong strands, while blowing air out of her mouth.

"Yeah. I'm good." As if they had a mind of their own, my fingers reached out and brushed the hair free.

"Thanks." She gave a happy sigh as she leaned back and rested her head on my shoulder.

My heart expanded against my rib cage, and I inhaled. Her perfume, the scent of her strawberry lip-gloss— everything Kate went to my head, leaving me dizzy. I shifted my arm, draping it behind her and curling my hand around her shoulder.

Jaden looked over her head, giving me a *what are you doing* type expression, and I silently sent one back telling him to mind his own business. Was it so bad to enjoy having her next to me for a short little ride? After we were out of the truck and in the boat I'd work on the distance thing.

We parked near the dock, and when Kate climbed out of the truck, she came my way, bumping into me when her jump down was slightly bigger than needed.

"Just so you know," I said, "if you try to knock me into the water today, I'm going to perform a ninja move and make sure you're the only one who falls in."

"Ooh, a ninja move. I'm so impressed, Space Case."

I shook my head. "You didn't."

"I did." She beamed at me.

"I'm never letting you speak to my mother again."

"Oh, come on. I like her. She promised baby pictures next time I came over."

"Another point for never letting you come over again." I narrowed my eyes at her. "Did she really?"

Kate laughed. "No, but your face was priceless." She jabbed a finger into my cheek. "And I do want to see the dimples on baby Cooper. It's got to be the cutest thing ever."

I playfully smacked her hand away, and she giggled and poked at my cheek again.

"Are we ever going to get in the water?" Jaden asked.

Kate glanced from him to me and gave a long-suffering sigh. "Oh great, two Coach Grouchy Pants to deal with. Just what I needed."

She started over to the boat, and I watched the sway of her hips, like I had that fateful day we'd struck our bargain.

She thought she had it bad with two rowers around to bark orders at her? I was falling for a girl who liked someone else.

Talk about just what I needed.

Chapter Nineteen

"But, Cooper, what if everyone there is mean? And what if I don't know what to say and I freeze up and ruin everything?" The closer the clock inched toward seven on Friday evening, the more frayed my nerves became. Yes, Mick and I'd had a few promising interactions and one decent conversation about college, but that just meant the stakes were that much higher if I blew it tonight.

"Then don't go," he said, and I scowled across the cab of his truck at him. He was being even more stubborn than usual.

"We had a deal."

"Hey, I got you invited over to Mick's house — I'm fulfilling my side. You were too distracted to row this afternoon, so if anyone should be complaining it's me."

I gasped. "You did not just say that to me."

"I did." He flashed me a smile, clearly thinking he was clever, using the words on me that I'd used on him yesterday. Once we rowed out on the lake with Jaden, Cooper had hardly spoken—Jaden gave me tips and we made a joke about how he could row the left side while I did the right. Cooper hadn't objected or told us to focus like I'd expected him to. He merely kept rowing, remaining far quieter than usual. Even during today's training sesh, he hadn't said much. He was careful not to bark orders, at least, but something was missing from our usual light banter. Sadness edged into his smile. "But I didn't mean it. I'm happy with our times this afternoon. As for tonight…you'll do fine, Kate. You've got this."

I gripped the handle above the window as he turned onto my road—the winter had turned it into half potholes, and the city didn't seem to be in any hurry to fill them. I wished life came with one of these "oh shit" handles so you could hold on to it when the road ahead turned bumpy. Cooper was the closest thing I had to one, and I liked having him nearby so I could cling on as needed. "I'd feel better if you came with me. Or, I guess that might give Mick the wrong idea, but can't you just show up?"

Cooper pulled into my driveway. Sunlight filtered through the trees and gave his profile a glowing effect. "It's not a big party. It'd be weird for me to show up."

Mick personally invited me, which was a huge freaking victory. We were just starting to get to know each other—to get to a place where he could see how much fun I could be and our connection could grow into more—and the pressure for everything to go perfectly weighed on me. History proved I didn't do the best under pressure. Or in Mick's presence. We're talking like 80 percent awkward, with a high chance of tripping over my words.

I could tell Cooper had made up his mind about not going, but that didn't mean he couldn't give me some extra tools to ensure success. "Can you at least help me pick out an outfit? Like I said, my mom has a late showing." Which was why I didn't have a vehicle to use and had that minor meltdown about how I finally got invited out with Mick, and I'd have to go over there all sweaty and gross, wearing the same clothes he'd seen me in at school.

Cooper eyed the door to my house as if going inside would be akin to going to battle. Maybe asking for fashion advice was too much—after all, he'd already offered to drop me off at Mick's so I could come home after training and freshen up. As I opened my mouth to tell him never mind, he said, "Okay. But only to say yay or nay. There will be no advice on accessories or makeup, and I will deny this ever happening."

"I hope you'll deny all of this ever happening. It's a top-secret operation, and the only people who have clearance are you and me."

He shook his head, but his smile turned genuine again. I dove across the cab of the truck and hugged him. "Thank you, Sergeant Callihan."

"You're going to be the death of me, Hamilton," he said, and I hugged him harder and added a smacking kiss on his cheek.

Even though it'd been an over-the-top cheesy gesture, I froze, worried awkwardness would creep in and he'd run screaming. Instead he laughed and put his hand on my back, and I got that fresh from the rollercoaster feeling.

Which I took as an omen that tonight was going to go well, and nothing more. Because I couldn't start having conflicted feelings about my secret mission partner right as I was about to land the guy I'd spent literally *years* crushing on.

That'd make things way too complicated, and the more complicated, the higher risk that I'd trip and fall on my face or butt. Then I'd end up lonely and alone, just like I was before Cooper and I made our deal.

• • •

"Are you sure you won't come in?" I asked Cooper when he pulled up in front of Mick's house.

"Remember how you said that would give Pecker the wrong idea?"

"But we could stagger our arrivals. It'd be so spy-like. We could make up badass call signs and secret signals…"

"You snagged his attention, Kate." Cooper's eyes flicked to me for the briefest moment. "And in that outfit, trust me, you'll keep it."

I swallowed, but my throat still felt too tight. And it's not like there was any fabric close to it, so it was definitely all nerves. Not that my clothing usually came up in the turtleneck range, but the slinky red tank with the tiny ribbon straps dipped lower than I was used to. "Are you sure the bright lipstick doesn't look silly?"

Cooper turned to me, the streetlight illuminating his eyes. "I'm sure."

"Okay." Expelling a long breath, I reached for the door handle.

"Kate?"

I spun back to face Cooper. He reached out, like he was going to put his hand on my cheek, but then he dropped it before it made contact. "If things go south, or you need a ride home, just call me."

Mick told me he'd give me a ride home when I talked to him at lunch earlier, but it was good to know I had such reliable backup. I nearly repeated my earlier move and kissed Cooper's cheek, but I didn't think I'd leave it at a smacking peck this time.

What's wrong with you? Do not *think about kissing Cooper, innocent cheek kiss or not.*

Still, I owed him, and I didn't think all the hours of rowing in the world could repay him. "Thank you. For everything." I almost licked my lips before stopping myself short of smearing my lipstick or ending up with some of it on my teeth. "You're a really good friend."

That earned me half a smile, one adorable dimple flashing in the cheek I'd almost kissed.

"And I'm not just saying that because you're my only friend," I added with a grin.

The other side of his mouth got in on the smile, both dimples nearly too much to handle. He reached out and squeezed my hand. "Right back at you. About the friend thing. I mean, I have other friends, but I can honestly say none of them are like you."

His gaze drifted behind me. "Someone's looking out the window. Better get in there."

"Yes, Coach."

I jumped out of the truck, and when I reached the step, I looked back and watched Cooper's truck drive away. It felt like a string in my chest was slowly unraveling, and I worried it'd snap once he got too far for me to see him.

But then I told myself to stop being a wimp and knocked on the door.

Chapter Twenty

COOPER

"Where've you been all week?" Dad asked the second I stepped in the door.

Every answer that popped into my mind would come out sarcastic, from "The lake," to "School," to "Here, where've you been?" Of course, that last one wasn't as innocent as the rest. "How's the case going?"

He pinched the bridge of his nose. "It's a mess, and a lot of damn paperwork, but it's going. Soon I'll have you to help sort through it, thank goodness. You could start the internship now, you know."

My skin tightened uncomfortably. This evening had already been hard enough, watching Kate head toward another guy in that sexy red top that was burned into my mind, right along with her lips.

Soft lips that'd pressed against my cheek earlier today.

No surprise, helping her choose an outfit was another exercise in torture. Since I had another crappy situation unfolding before me, I focused on it. "With school and everything, it'd be better to wait until after graduation."

"You don't need to spend every second on the lake," Dad said, tossing a thick file on top of another one. "Growing up means taking on responsibilities."

"I know. I appreciate everything you and Mom have done for me. I just need another couple of months."

Mom wandered in. "Give him a break, Paul."

"And I should listen to you because you work hard to pay all the bills around here?"

Mom went ramrod straight, offense clear on her features.

Dad held up a hand. "I'm sorry. That was out of line. I know you work hard maintaining the house and with your organizations. I'm just stressed about this case."

He was never *not* stressed about a case, be it this one, or the hundreds of others he'd had through the years, or even ones that might come up. And that was the life he wanted for me, the path he couldn't even reasonably discuss without giving ultimatums and whipping out our entire family history going back three generations. He spoke sharply all the time, and I wondered if that'd be me someday, rude to the point of mean, only to blame stressful cases.

Kate already claims I'm that way with rowing. I tried not to be, but maybe she did deserve some airhead dude who would just drool over her while putting his hands—

I stopped that line of thinking before I ended up pissed off enough to jump right into a fight with my dad and tell him exactly what I thought of his internship and being a lawyer.

Chapter Twenty-One

KATE

The first thing I noticed was the tall, raven-haired girl with sharp features who had her arm around Mick.

Shock and disappointment bolted my feet to the floor, which was super inconvenient considering the urge to flee also overwhelmed me.

Mick's gaze swept the room, and he did a double take when he looked my way. The smirk that tilted his mouth gave me heart palpitations, and seriously, why did my emotions all crash into each other whenever I was near him? "Kate. Hey."

He left the model-esque female at his side—since I didn't recognize her, I assumed she didn't go to our school, but maybe that was only my low standing on the social ladder—and approached me. He ran his eyes up and down me. "Damn you look sexy."

Heat flared in my cheeks. "Thank you. You, too."

He put his hand on my back and led me over to the table, where four guys were already seated. A handful of other people milled around the room, including the raven-haired girl who would fry me on the spot if she had laser vision. "Have you played poker before?"

"I know the general rules, but I've only watched a few games on TV."

"Then you can watch me play." He sat down and pulled me onto his lap. "You can be my good luck charm," he whispered in my ear and a pleasant chill traveled down my spine.

When the boys started throwing cash on the table, it took everything in me to not gasp at the amount—I could buy a ton of Funko Pop figurines with that kind of dough. After I got over my initial shock, it didn't take long to get into the flow of the game.

Mick leaned forward to bet, and I put my hand on his chest. Everyone stared at me, most likely wondering why I was holding up the show. I almost abandoned my attempt to warn him, but I couldn't help it. I moved my lips next to his ear and whispered, "The odds of you beating the guy at the end of the table are super low. Like fifteen percent. So if I were you, I'd either fold or bluff big." I sat up enough to look into his face. I bit my lip. "Or ignore me, what do I know?"

Mick studied me for a moment, and the scrutiny made me squirm, which almost made me fall off his lap—laps weren't all that comfortable in terms of long-term seating, FYI. Not that I'd abandon the spot I had wanted to be in forever, but I found it surprising.

I don't remember feeling that way when I fell onto Cooper's lap. I quickly swatted away the unbidden thought, but then I heard Cooper's voice talking about how he was a ninja, and why did my brain hate me?

"I fold," Mick said, tossing his cards.

Sure enough, the guy at the end of the table won. He glared at Mick and me. "So now you're a cheater?"

"I'm simply utilizing my good luck charm," Mick said,

wrapping his arms around me and pulling me to his chest. Again, it felt like we'd passed the beginning get-to-know you phase and moved right into full-contact dating. But since I'd dreamed of that very thing, I couldn't pinpoint why I couldn't simply relax and go with it better.

Maybe because I added that "what do I know" comment after I gave him sound statistics advice, like I needed to hide just how much I do know.

At the guy's deepening scowl, Mick patted my leg. "Looks like someone's going to be a baby about losing. Why don't you go get a drink? Maybe grab me one, too? If you don't mind?"

I twisted to face Mick and decided to stop overanalyzing everything and embrace how far I'd come. After all, he'd called me his good luck charm, and I was sure I'd get used to this warp speed intimacy in time. Maybe if I threw myself fully into it, too? I played with the ends of his hair—or tried— there wasn't much to play with, not like Cooper's, and that one section that constantly fell in his face. "Sure. I'll be right back."

Once I reached the basement bar area, I took the chance to catch my breath. I pulled out my phone, wanting to send Cooper a text and tell him I thought I was doing even better than expected.

But the fact that I'd thought about his lap and his jokes— and his freaking hair—stopped me. Maybe I was spending too much time with him, and that was why everything got all mixed up and muddy in my head.

So I pocketed my phone and grabbed two drinks.

And when I returned to the table to see Mick was now standing, the raven-haired girl's hand on his arm as she talked to him, I was rather proud that I didn't drop them.

By the end of the first round of poker, one thing was clear. I wasn't the only girl in Mick's rotation. *You knew he averaged four girls a semester.*

Yeah, but I didn't know it was closer to two girls a night.

That last interaction looked more like she initiated it, though.

Since my options were either admit defeat, or work harder to show him how right we were for each other, I sat my butt down at the poker table and asked if I could play.

The twenty-dollar buy-in made my gut drop, but I told myself to trust my calculator brain. Within the hour, I made two hundred dollars and received dozens of impressed looks and compliments from Mick.

The tall model chick gave up halfway through and went to flirt with Vance Mitchell instead. I couldn't help but give an internal fist pump. *Winning at poker, and winning at boys. This certainly is an interesting turn of events…*

I gathered my winnings into a pile. "Thanks for letting me play. I'm going to bow out now." No way was I going to play until I lost everything.

Mick leaned in, his hand on my thigh. "Are you some kind of pool shark?"

I laughed. "No." To keep or not to keep my secret? The idea was to reveal the real me a little at a time, right? *Besides, "serious" and "smart" are two different things, and I'm not going to play dumb to try to make someone like me.* "I'm good at calculating odds, though—math and statistics are kind of my thing." I lowered my voice and bent closer. "Pissy Poker Player doesn't look too happy about it."

Mick chuckled and wrapped his hand tighter around my thigh. "Pissy Poker Player can deal. I think I should take you and your card counting to Vegas."

Card counting? Was that what I was doing? That was illegal, wasn't it? I almost felt bad enough to give back the money I'd made, but I took in Pissy Poker Player's clothing and the fat designer watch that was totally for show, and decided he could afford it. Plus, my classified Operation was well under way and making progress, and I needed money for a prom dress.

Mick scooted away from the table. "I've got to circulate a bit. Will you be okay on your own?"

"Yeah. Mind if I look around?"

Mick kissed the spot under my ear and whispered, "Knock yourself out."

If he knew that I'd wondered countless times what his bedroom looked like, he probably would've thought twice about granting me an all access pass. Since I could hear Cooper telling me the name I'd put Mick under in my phone would make the guy freak — something I still needed to change — I figured going through his room was also a no-no.

I stuck to the lower level, and a few minutes into my mini, self-guided tour, I bumped into Amber. She smiled and said "hey," so I figured I'd attempt the polite conversation I hadn't gotten around to the other day. "Hey, back. I didn't know you were here."

"Just decided to swing by last minute — I waitress at MoeJoe's now, so if I smell like food, that's why."

"Fun. I mean, the waitressing, not smelling like food. Not that you do." I couldn't help glancing around her, steeling myself for the dirty looks I'd get from the rest of her crew if they were also on their way in.

"Paris isn't with me."

"Oh. I didn't…" Know how to finish. Words didn't come easy between us anymore, which was sad, because at one point, we'd talked for hours on end.

"Anyway, Jared called to see if I'd bring him a burger and fries, like the mooch he is." She rolled her eyes as she held up a white bag. "Guess I better go find him and tell him he owes me a really big tip."

I nodded, not bothering to point her in any direction, because I didn't know who Jared was. Idly I wondered if she was dating him. If she was happy. A dozen other ifs that flickered quickly through my mind.

Amber hesitated, then seemed to abandon whatever she was going to say and simply gave me another smile before heading toward the group of people in the living room.

I continued to the other side of the room and ended up in front of a massive window overlooking the backyard. The lake sat just beyond that, the water as dark as an oil spill with the sun fully set.

Occasionally I spotted Mick in the crowd, and he was always a little too friendly with the girls for my liking, but a lot of the time, they were the ones who initiated the flirty touches, and he and I weren't an official thing.

Hopefully soon, though. If I play my cards right, and tonight proved that I'm rather good at cards. A smug sense of victory made me feel light and floaty.

The twinkling stars in the inky sky caught my eye and I searched out the constellations Cooper had shown me. *Is that Hercules? Or is it that other star cluster?*

Honestly, none of them looked like a dude standing on a dragon, and I couldn't recognize anything besides the Big Dipper.

Arms wound around my waist, and I stiffened. Then relaxed at the sound of Mick's voice. "There you are. I was looking for you." He swept my hair off the back of my neck and pressed his lips there.

My pulse raced, and heat flooded my body. *This is it. I'm going to kiss Mick. Something magical will happen, and everything will change, and before you know it, we'll be walking into a decorated gym, him in a tux and me in a sparkly dress.*

But when I spun in his arms, I noticed how many people

were nearby and looking our way.

I didn't want twenty people to witness our first kiss.

My muscles tensed back up. *Say we do kiss. Will it be all over school come Monday? What will people call us? Kick. Mate. Ugh, our names don't do a very good job of merging in a cute way. How have I never noticed that before?*

Why am I freaking noticing it now?

"Everything okay?" Mick asked, doing a full-body lean that pressed me against the glass. Suddenly I was wondering how much weight it could hold, because it'd so be my luck to break right through and come out of this entire thing covered in cuts and glass shards.

"It's just… I…" I ran my hand through my hair. "Could we talk?"

His face scrunched up like I'd suggested a lemon-sucking contest, but then his features smoothed. "Of course. You want to go somewhere more private?"

Yes. But wait. Isn't that hookup code? While I wanted privacy, I didn't want to get into a situation I wasn't ready for. Anxiety rose, priming me to say or do something stupid and undo everything.

"Maybe we could just sit over there?" I gestured to the loveseat not quite in the center of the action, but not out of it, either. And it was a loveseat, which meant sitting close, and I hoped he'd be okay with that being all we did tonight.

"Oh-kay." The hesitation clear on his face came through in his voice.

Obviously I was already undoing everything, crashing into shore before I even got our ship fully launched. But there was harmless pretending and doing something I couldn't take back, and while my lines might've been shaky recently, there were ones I wouldn't cross just to get a guy.

Even if the guy was Mick Pecker, all-star quarterback and object of my obsession and covert operation.

Once we sat down, he folded my hand in his, helping my shaky confidence regain its legs. "It was pretty funny how you beat Jared. He almost always wins the games."

"Who? Oh, Pissy Poker Player." Mick laughed, and I threw my free hand over my mouth. "Sorry, that's so rude of me to call him that." In the name of goodwill or whatever—if that was what Amber and my earlier conversation was about—I should especially stop if she and he were a thing. From what I'd seen at my post at the window, it looked more friendly than relationshipy.

"I like it. I always thought you were a more serious girl, or I would've talked to you a lot earlier."

"Me? Serious?" I shrugged, and apparently I didn't do that much, because it felt like a foreign movement my body didn't know how to naturally do. Or maybe Mick's full attention just psyched me out too much.

How often do I shrug? Cooper does it all the time.

Gah, focus, Kate! Focus!

"Honestly, it's more that I'm kind of shy." I looked up, and my heart skipped a beat when I peered into his blue, blue eyes. "It takes me a little while to warm up and be myself around people."

Mick slipped his fingers between mine. "Well, I think that's cute."

"More like inconvenient and awkward, but I like cute better."

"You're funny, too," Mick said with a smile, and a swirl of excitement went through my gut. "So, I haven't told anyone besides my family yet, but I thought about what you said about colleges—and airplanes"—he squeezed my hand—"and I'm going to go to Penn State. I turned in my letter of intent to the coach today."

"Really? That's so cool. And you don't need to worry about the competition. You'll take them out—in a nice way, of course—no problem."

"Of course," he said, amusement flickering through his eyes. And even though it was silly, I couldn't help thinking that seven hours wasn't such a long drive if things progressed over summer—I was too poor for airplanes.

He told me his little brother understood and said he'd be cheering for him, and then we moved on to discussing summer plans. Mick was planning on training and doing a lot of swimming and kayaking, and I replied that I'd like to do some kayaking, too, since it was something I'd never done before. He generously offered to help me with that.

Everything progressed nicely from there, all those get-to-know-you blanks I felt like we skipped slowly getting filled in. It wasn't quite as smooth or entertaining as the conversations Cooper and I had, but because of our history and becoming even closer friends the past few weeks, naturally that would happen, so I wasn't sure why my brain even decided to bring it up.

Especially since I already knew we had a good time together, just like I knew Cooper and I didn't feel the same about a lot of things. Like how there were fun activities not involving rowing or the lake, and how necessary it was to train "all out, 100 percent of the time." We definitely had a different outlook on grades and school in general…oh, and prom—that was a *big* one. He thought it was just some silly dance that required too much time and effort, and I still couldn't believe he didn't even want to go.

His loss, because it's going to be amazing.

If I stop getting distracted by random thoughts and focus on whatever Mick's saying now so I can ensure I have the perfect date, that is.

By the time the party started winding down, Mick and I were clicking rather well, enough so that I almost brought up prom. Just straight-up asked if he had a date already, and if not, would he go with me.

But then the raven-haired beauty came to say good-bye, her body language speaking of either a past she and Mick had or a future she hoped they'd have, and I felt like I needed a little more time to show him how awesome I was before I asked him to spend one of the most important, memorable nights of high school as my date.

Chapter Twenty-Two

The last person I wanted to see first thing Monday morning was Pecker, but as my shitty luck would have it, there he stood.

Clearly he wanted to talk to me, which made me want to slow my pace even more. "Hey, Callihan," he said.

"Hey," I said, dragging out the word. Hopefully he got the message that this situation was odd, and I'd rather he get it over with or go away. Preferably option two.

He glanced around and took a step closer. "I wanted to ask you a question about Kate."

Every muscle coiled tight; my breath froze in my lungs. "What about her?" While I tried to cover the tension in my body, my voice came out sharp.

His forehead crinkled up. "Wait. You and she aren't a thing, are you? I asked her."

Would it make a difference? The temptation to tell him to stay away from her was strong, but he was who she wanted. Claiming her would only make her a bigger challenge as far as he was concerned anyway. "We're friends."

"I've always thought she was pretty, but I thought she was one of those serious, all about the rules girls, so I kept my distance. But I still can't quite figure her out. You guys ever… mess around?"

The pencil in my hand snapped and I gritted my teeth. "You're asking about my sex life? What? The cable not working at your house, Pecker?"

He clenched his jaw. "Never mind. Jeez, I forgot what a prick you could be."

Well, I hadn't forgotten what a prick he could be.

But then I thought about Kate and what she wanted, and I was trying not to screw up her plans, even as all my instincts told me to. "She's smart, so everyone thinks she's serious, but there's a big difference." As I said it, I realized how true it was. I'd never laughed the way I did with her. She wouldn't even let me be too serious—she pushed me to slow down and have fun.

Before I got distracted with thoughts of all the fun we'd had, and that afternoon we'd ended up *in* the lake, I charged on. "She's funny and sweet, and she's one of the best people I know. It's none of my business what you two do, just like it's none of yours what she and I do."

Was I really going to add the rest? Seal the deal with the act we'd set up and then get the hell out of this crazy scheme? At this point, it might be the only way I ever slept again—I definitely hadn't this past weekend, wondering how far Kate took her mission. "The truth is, I wouldn't mind getting more serious, but she's all about just having fun. With graduation and college coming up, she doesn't want to be tied down."

Pecker looked way too pleased about that news. Helping Kate land her crush didn't feel like a challenge anymore. It was more akin to slow, drawn-out torture. In fact, I think I'd rather have someone tear out my fingernails one by one. At least that would end eventually, because I only had so many fingers.

"So please," I said, "screw up. I'm cheering for you to be an ass, because then she'll realize she'd be better off with just me."

That last part wasn't part of the plan, it just came out. But the truth of it reverberated through me. I'd done my best to give Kate what she wanted. Now all I could do was hope that the tool in front of me screwed it up so that maybe I could get her to see me.

But I wasn't gonna hold my breath.

• • •

For the next few days, I avoided Kate as much as I could. I texted her and told her I couldn't do the rowing thing because I had some family stuff to take care of.

She'd texted back that she couldn't believe I actually knew what it meant to take a break from training, family stuff or not.

In spite of how much I wanted to, I didn't text her back. Instead I forced myself to dwell on the image of her in the school hall with Pecker's arm around her; of them sitting close during lunch—their cuddling sessions were burned into my brain anyway, so I figured I might as well use them for good.

When I noticed her seated at the edge of the parking lot on Thursday afternoon—in the very same spot I'd seen her in a few weeks back—I told myself to climb in my truck and leave as fast as I could.

Of course my body didn't listen, automatically angling toward her.

Our eyes met, and she flashed me a sad smile that nearly dropped me to my knees. Without thinking, I rushed over. "What happened? Did he hurt you?"

Her eyebrows pulled together. "He?"

"Pec—Mick."

She pressed her lips into a flat line like she was fighting her emotions, and I decided I'd kill him. Ironic that I'd need a good lawyer afterward, but I'd think about that later. "*You're* hurting me," she said.

My blood froze in my veins, the shift from anger to guilt giving my internal organs whiplash.

She reached up and twisted a strand of hair around her finger. "I saw you on the lake yesterday after school, when I was with Mick. Was I not fast enough?"

The way her voice cracked made my chest ache.

"I thought I was getting better at the rowing thing, but I'll work on it," she said, her pleading eyes wide. "I'll be more serious about your training from now on, I promise. I'll even try to refrain from calling you Coach Grouchy Pants, no matter how tempted I am."

I shook my head. "It's not you."

"Really?" Her features hardened, that unexpected fiery side of her rising to the surface—and God help me, it sent a dart of desire right through me. "You're going to use a pathetic break-up type line on me? You know that everyone who's ever said that is full of crap."

I raked my fingers through my hair, trying to decide whether to let it go or engage. After all, I'd kept my part of the bargain the other day and told Mick what he wanted to hear. Despite how hard I'd tried to stay out of the drama, I'd ended up in the thick of it, because of this girl. In some ways, cutting my losses and focusing on my original goal of more time on the lake and not let anything else get in the way would be the smart play.

But leaving things strained between Kate and me? It'd eat away at me, and trying to ignore her had already left me feeling raw for days. Surrendering to the crazy magnetic pull she had on me, I stepped over the curb and moved to sit, but I had to bump her with my hip to clear enough room. "I'm not breaking up with you. I just needed space."

"Well, remember how I told you that you're my only friend? No pressure, but I need my friend." A contemplative crinkle creased her forehead. "Okay, I guess that's pressure, but you know what, I don't care. You don't get to just blow me off with a lame claim of needing space. Friends talk to each other." She crossed her arms, her expression all business. "So talk."

I wanted to tell her that her logic was flawed, but I couldn't exactly explain why I needed space without confessing a whole lot more. Like how I couldn't stop thinking about her, everything from her laugh to her smile to her fandom talk. How I didn't want her to hang around with Pecker anymore, because I wanted her to pick me instead.

Talk about a good way to end a friendship. Since she'd pointed out I was all she had in that area, it'd make me a huge jerk to let my selfish wants eclipse what she wanted. Especially since she'd been clear about hers from the very beginning.

I rubbed the back of my neck and glanced around— evidently the paranoid tables had turned. She was talking freely, and I worried about eavesdroppers. "How about we head to the lake, but not for rowing. Just to be there and have fun and forget everything else for a while?"

She blinked at me.

"Unless you're waiting for Mick?"

"Yes. I mean no. I mean, no I'm not waiting for Mick, and yes to heading to the lake. Let me just text my mom and tell her I've got a ride home. Assuming you'll take me home after?"

I almost slipped and made it crystal clear as to how I felt about her by telling her I'd take her anywhere she wanted me to.

Chapter Twenty-Three

KATE

I told myself to just be happy that Cooper and I were finally talking again, but there was some invisible presence in the cab of the truck with us. Not like an actual ghost or paranormal being. More like everything left unsaid crowded the space and made it hard to know what to actually say.

The past few days completely freaked me out, and I'd been sure Cooper was about to pull an Amber on me and just phase me out of his life like it wasn't a big deal. The same eclipsing sense of loneliness hit me full force, and I'd had trouble sleeping. I worried I'd come on too strong or done something wrong, and I didn't want to do anything that would mess up our friendship. I wasn't sure how I became so attached after only a little over two weeks of consistently hanging out, but I had, and I needed us to be okay with a desperation I hadn't felt since losing my dad.

I tapped my fingers on my leg, trying to come up with something to fill the quickly-turning-awkward silence. When

I thought I recognized the song on the radio, I reached over and turned it up. "Hmm."

"What?" Cooper asked.

"At first I thought this was the song they played during one of the Haylijah scenes on *The Originals*, but it's not."

"This is the same show you named your pet dragon after?"

Warmth tingled through me. *He remembered.* "Yeah. Even Klaus—the vampire version—ships them, which is complicated since she had his baby. I was hoping after Elijah and Hayley hooked up, which I waited for-seriously-ever for, we could get to the canon stage, but of course it's not that easy."

"To shoot a cannon?" His expression read as serious, but the teasing tone made it clear he knew that wasn't what I meant.

"A canon's a ship that's been confirmed by the series."

"Okay."

"You're fighting the urge to call me crazy now, aren't you? I can see it in the little twitch in your cheek." I wanted to poke one of his dimples, like I'd done before, but with our friendship in barely-getting-back-to-normal territory, I didn't know if it'd cross a line. "Don't try to deny it, because last weekend I found out I'm really good at poker. I made a couple hundred dollars off Mick and his friends—enough for a prom dress, I hope."

The twitch I'd pointed out took hold and a smile curved his lips. "You hustled those guys out of their money? Let me guess, you used mathematical deviousness?"

"Hey, I didn't choose the math thug life, it chose me."

Cooper's laugh bounced across the cab and the happy sound echoed through my chest. "I'm so proud. And for the first time, I'm actually regretting not crashing that night."

All that suffocating unsaid stuff lifted, and then we were

back to Kate and Cooper, friends who understood each other, even when we didn't.

Naturally I questioned that theory when Cooper pulled two fishing poles out from behind the seat of his truck.

"Um, what's that all about?" I gestured to the poles, making a circle to encompass them.

"We're going to just enjoy the lake, remember?"

"By fishing?"

"Put your nose back where it belongs," he said, making me realize I'd scrunched it up. "It's going to be fun. Don't tell me you haven't fished before."

"Okay, I won't tell you."

His eyes widened. "For real?"

"My dad used to go now and then, but I acted as his assistant rower. I refused to put a pole in the water, because I didn't want to hook any poor little fishies."

"That explains why you can row. You could move the boat with him in it?"

"Not very far," I admitted. "But I was determined to try so that he'd take me. He was gone a lot, even when he wasn't deployed, so if I had the opportunity to go anywhere with him, I jumped on it. Even if it meant fish might be flopping around on the floor of the boat at my feet. He used to tease me by swinging them toward me and asking me to unhook them, or picking one up and talking on his behalf, always about how honored he'd be to serve as our dinner."

Memories from those lazy days with my dad on the lake flickered through my mind. His goofy floppy hat, the empty Dr Pepper cans in the middle of the boat that acted as a measure for how long we'd been out on the water, and how we always returned home sunburned but happy. "One day I surprised him by granting his request to unhook a fish, only to release the slimy thing back in the water and tell him to swim away as fast as he could and not to fall for food that seemed too good to be true. I thought my dad might get a little upset, but he just laughed and told me I was still his favorite fishing partner."

Cooper's voice softened. "You don't talk about him much."

"Probably because I worry if I do, then I might cry, and that'd be embarrassing." Over the past few days I'd thought about him a lot, as if my mind was incapable of missing anyone without remembering who else I missed.

Cooper reached out and brushed his fingers across my cheek. "Not embarrassing. You lost someone."

My heart swelled and tears clogged my throat. "He was my hero. We used to go on these made-up missions together—which is probably why I'm enjoying this one with you so much. We'd pretend people we passed on the street were spies and plot how we'd take down their evil organization. We also went on real missions, where we'd go shopping to find the perfect present for my mom, which usually involved another salt and pepper shaker for her collection. Stuff like that."

Cooper ran his fingers down my arm and squeezed my hand. "He sounds awesome."

"He was." My voice faltered and I worked to put more sound behind it. "After he passed away, the only thing that made me feel better was binge watching TV and cheering for those characters' happy endings. I'd always been prone to fandom tendencies, but that definitely moved them into overdrive."

"Confession time?" Cooper raised an eyebrow. "It's one of the things I like most about you. Even if I don't understand half of what you say."

I hugged him around the middle, and the fishing poles clattered to the ground when he wrapped his arms around me and hugged me back. "Look, I've already been abandoned by a friend, and it really hurt. So I know this is super selfish, but could you please not need space ever again?"

He tucked his chin on top of my head. "Right now, the last thing I'm thinking about is space. Between us, or the space that's over our head and in a distant galaxy far, far away. And that's saying something."

I laughed and pulled back so I could look him in the eye. "I like your obsession with space, and I also like that you're equally obsessed with boats and water."

"Obsession? I'd call them more…mild infatuations."

"Just take the compliment, Callihan."

He lifted one finger and gave me a mini-salute. "Aye, aye, Hamilton."

Chapter Twenty-Four

COOPER

Since Kate would liberate any fish we caught and it wasn't her thing anyway, I switched gears and pulled the Jet Ski out of the shed.

I drove us out on the middle of the lake, and it was possible I'd driven a bit faster and made sharper turns than usual because it meant she held on tighter to me. Her little squeals of excitement also heated my blood and egged me on.

Man, I'd missed her. It seemed like we'd been apart weeks instead of days, and being out on the lake with her again only made me want the day to never end.

I slowed and let the waves determine our path as I looked over my shoulder at her. Water droplets clung to her hair and lashes and her cheeks were pink and wind whipped. "What do you think?"

Kate rubbed her hands together. "That it's my turn to drive."

We switched places and she leaned forward and gripped

the rubber handles. I waited for us to move. After a few seconds, she glanced back at me. "Yeah, I've never done this before."

"Oh. I got you." I reached around her, and my cheek brushed hers as I placed my hands over hers. "Reverse on the left"—I demonstrated—"forward on the right, and squeeze for brakes. Got it?"

Her eyes remained on mine; I forgot how to breathe. "Maybe one more time," she said, and the breathlessness in her voice implied she wasn't totally unaffected by our closeness. Or maybe my imagination was getting carried away.

I cleared my throat and went over everything again.

"Okay, I've got it," she said. "You better hold on."

"Just promise that if your crazy driving makes me fall off, you'll come back for me."

"I would've before that crazy driving comment; now you're on your own." With that, she punched the gas. We jolted forward, and I realized I should've taken it out of sports mode. At her happy whoop, I decided to let it ride. She made a few wide circles, and then the wind picked up, making the waves choppy.

We bounced our way back to shore, and I took over the controls once we were a few feet away. I climbed off the Jet Ski, then helped Kate down, my hands lingering on her waist longer than needed.

But she didn't pull away. "Thanks. That was fun."

Once everything was put back in the shed, I sat down on the grass near the shore. Kate lowered herself next to me and started pulling up clumps. I needed to remind myself that she and I weren't a possibility again, because every time I was around her, I tended to forget. Or perhaps I simply wanted to forget.

"So, how are things going with Mick?" I asked, doing my best not to cringe. "You guys hanging out a lot?"

"No. Just the poker night and then yesterday we went for a hike with some of his friends. I've got more competition than I realized, but it's going…okay. I think."

"Well, that's good."

She nodded and formed her clumps of grass into a nest. "I'm still afraid to broach the prom topic, but since we're pretty much at four weeks and counting, it's only a matter of time before someone asks him, or he asks someone, and I'm not sure he'd choose me right now."

"He'd be an idiot not to."

She smiled. "Thanks. But we didn't come here to discuss the Operation. Today it doesn't exist."

I wanted to say good, and then pull her into my arms and kiss her. See if I couldn't get it to not exist ever again. *You're trying not to ruin the friendship, remember?*

She'd made it clear that I was her only friend and that she needed me, and while she'd jokingly added "no pressure," I felt it. Because I needed her, too, more than I realized. Kissing her would change everything, and the risk of messing up our friendship was too high. Especially when I factored in how her endgame of taking Mick to prom obviously hadn't changed. I'd like to think I'd be big enough to smother the rejection and continue to be her friend regardless, but I knew it'd be too hard if we crossed that line.

"I want to talk about you." Kate grabbed my hand and my throat went dry as I tried to remind myself of all the reasons I'd vetoed crossing the line. "I can tell something's weighing on you, and I think it has to do with your dad."

Damn. The girl saw right through me. "It's nothing."

"No, it's not." She bumped her shoulder into mine. "This is what friends are for. To listen to you vent or rant, and to be on your side, no matter what."

There it was. Another mention of us being friends. Shoving away my conflicted feelings over that, I ran a hand through my hair and allowed the frustration I experienced whenever I thought about my dad and the future he insisted on to take center stage. "He wants me to be a lawyer."

Kate wrinkled her nose the way she'd done when I mentioned fishing. "A lawyer? I can't imagine you being a lawyer. You'd probably charm everyone into letting you win, but still...You? In an office wearing a suit? It doesn't compute."

"All the men in my family are lawyers. I feel ungrateful, because his success has given me a pretty cushy life." I felt even more ungrateful knowing that Kate and her mom worked so hard for their life. That she worried about how to pay for a prom dress—I liked that she'd outplayed Pecker and his friends to help her with that, though. "But he gets more and more stressed the bigger the case, and if you think I get grouchy, I've got nothing on him. It's like he's the guy I remember from my childhood only once every few months, and I know my mom feels it, too.

"He's already set me up with an internship with his firm this summer, and then college will start, and... I don't mind working, but I want to keep on rowing, and I'm interested in several fields. I'd like a chance to explore them and see what I really want to do."

"What fields? Astronomy?"

"That's one of them," I said, and the fact that she knew me so well helped soothe my frustration. "You called me obsessed with the water, but I'm also pretty obsessed with what's in it. I'd love to study marine biology and do something in that field. It'd keep me on the water a lot, which is my favorite place to be."

"Now that...?" Kate studied me, and she even added a chin stroke, as if she were super deep in thought. "That fits. You should talk to your dad about what you really want to do."

Just the thought sent trepidation through me. He'd yell, my mom would try to get involved, and then he'd declare his word the end all, be all, and we'd have to live with the even grumpier version of him. "He'd freak if I so much as mentioned the idea of changing degrees. I've tried to hint at it a few times, and even that's enough to make him get all grouchy and shut down any further attempts at talking about it. He's got my entire college and career planned out and I haven't even started yet."

"So what? You're going to go to college, get a law degree, and become a lawyer to make him happy? When are you going to live *your* life?"

"I'm not sure I can afford to live my life—he won't pay for school if I change degrees, I'm sure of it. And Harvard isn't exactly known for being cheap. But they have the best rowing team—the best marine biology program, too."

"I know I'll have to take out student loans to even attend a state school, but I hear it's still doable."

The way she laid it out made it seem so simple.

She spread the grass she'd formed into a nest, scattering it in a stripe in front of her, and then slapping her hands together. "Sorry. I'm not being supportive of your rant. What I mean to say is, *that sucks!* You should get to do what you want!"

I shot her a grin. "I actually appreciate the more logical counterpoints."

"Oh no. Counterpoints? The brainwashing lawyers have gotten to you already." She gripped my shirt dramatically. "Come back to me, Space Case. Don't let them have you."

"If anyone's been body-snatched, I think it might be you."

She laughed. Then her expression turned serious. "Have you ever thought that a completely honest conversation with your dad, even if it's a hard one, might clear this all up?"

"I tried at the beginning of the year. He shut it down. He

told me about how he was hesitant at first, too, but that his father and his grandfather were lawyers, and now he's glad his father made him see reason. Oh, and he made sure to throw in a mention about how I'm his only son, and how it's my job to carry on the Callihan name at the Callihan, Anderson, and Smith law firm in Manchester."

"Well, counselor. If you don't want to be forced into a career you don't want, you might have to put up a better argument. As a lawyer, surely he'll appreciate that." She curled her fingers around mine. "And just know that I'll be here for you afterward, no matter how it goes."

In the end, that might be the only thing that gave me enough courage to try.

Chapter Twenty-Five

KATE

Okay, I so didn't want to be that girl who stared at her phone all day waiting for a boy to call. Unfortunately, I *was* that girl last night. I could hardly even enjoy *Arrow* because I kept turning it down, thinking I'd heard my phone.

How dare Mick make me miss the show with my OTP!

But by Saturday morning, I'd decided I was as much to blame as he was. A phone worked two ways, after all, and I lived in a day and age where a girl could call up a guy. According to Mom, I should be thanking her generation for that.

So after showering and getting ready for the day, I went to my bedroom, closed the door behind me, and scooped up Klaus. I set him on my lap and petted his head as I took in all my paired figurines. Only one way to get a prom picture that'd look awesome in the mix, and that was to go after what I wanted.

I wonder if Cooper talked to his dad about what he *wants.*

After I made this phone call, I'd check in with my on-again friend. Yesterday proved how much better my life was with him in it. Being able to talk about my dad with Cooper had soothed the ache of missing him, and I loved how we could easily go from that to joking around to Jet Skiing at ridiculously fast speeds to discussing his rocky relationship with his dad. Loved how he'd confided in me about what he truly wanted to study in college. Even in the best times with Amber, we'd never gotten deep like that.

I'm going to do whatever it takes to make sure our friendship stays that way.

Panic squeezed my lungs at the thought of him suddenly dropping me the way Amber had, even as I assured myself he wouldn't, especially after I told him how much it would hurt me. Our friendship was stronger; it would last.

At least until he had to go to Harvard in the fall.

The squeezing sensation returned, and I worried what I'd do when he left. I'd be alone again…

Okay, no reason to freak out over something that's still months away. I took a few deep yoga-type breaths, a trick I'd learned when my overthinking ways got the best of me, and redirected, another tool that came in handy.

Cooper and I are good again, so I need to focus on getting that prom picture to add to my shelves.

For one blip of a second, I saw Cooper standing next to me in a tux instead of Mick. My stomach dipped, my pulse quickened, and a thread of desire stitched its way through my core, the same way it had when he showed me how to work the Jet Ski, his lips a mere breath from mine.

Then my carefully laid plans began shouting at me for trying to mess them up, a jumbled tangle of clashing, confusing thoughts tumbling around in my mind.

Speaking of messing things up, I'd just vowed to do whatever it took to ensure Cooper and I stayed good friends, and now I was tempting fate by entertaining dangerous, more-than-friends thoughts about him?

Immediately, the logical side of my brain came to my defense. *It's okay. Friends sometimes go to prom together…*

I'd spent a lot of time picturing it as a big romantic night with slow dancing and kissing, and part of me didn't want to let that go, even though I knew Cooper and I would definitely have fun.

Correction: *I* would have fun. Cooper made it clear he didn't want to go to prom. He'd even said it was a lot of effort for a night he'd just forget in a few years, so basically he didn't understand the point at all, and I didn't want him to go with me out of pity.

Deciding I was simply psyching myself out and maybe even doing some self-sabotage so I wouldn't have to risk possibly getting rejected, I looked down at my notebook with my detailed Operation. It had gotten me this far. I just needed to take those last few steps.

Then I'd have an awesome friend I could have low-key hangouts with *and* the perfect prom date, and I could declare the end of my senior year a raging success.

Not allowing myself any more time to second-guess my decision, I hit the little telephone next to Mick's name, and the phone rang.

And rang.

And rang.

"You've got Mick. Leave me a message."

My blood pressure skyrocketed. Clearly I should've prepared for this option. The beep made me jump. "Hey, 'sup?" *Oh my gosh, did I really just use "'sup?"* "Anywho," I said, because I couldn't stop saying the wrong thing. "I was wondering what you were up to today. And tonight. Really, either one."

Abort, abort, abort…

"Guess I'll catch up with you later." I hit end, then flopped onto my bed face-down and groaned into the pillow. Why had I gone all guns blazing and called him instead of sending an editable text? Boldness was totally overrated.

My phone rang and I jerked up. *He called me back!*

Only it wasn't Mick. Cooper's name flashed across my display instead.

A flutter of excitement went through my tummy, and I took one quick second to make sure my emotions were in check before answering. "Hey, Space Case."

"I'll give you that one, but I want a new nickname, stat."

"I'll get right on it. Oh, and I know you can't see me, but I'm saluting you right now." I saluted nobody, because not doing it seemed like lying, and guilt came after me for stupid reasons. "How do you feel about Aquaman?"

"Well, I've seen the preview for the upcoming movie with him in it, and our bodies are equally as ripped, so…"

"You're at a six on the Kanye scale, so I'd stop there. Honestly, I'd put it higher, but since I was the one foolish enough to compare you to the superhero, I knocked off a few points."

"Wow, you're so generous today," Cooper said. "Speaking of today, what are you up to?"

"Nothing much."

"I was thinking of heading to downtown Manchester to see what trouble I could get into. You wanna go with?"

As badly as I wanted to go, I almost said no, just in case Mick called—I really needed to amp things up if I was going to ask him to prom this next week. Not to mention the lapse in judgment I'd had over where exactly the friends line was a couple of minutes ago.

But the thought of saying no, only to sit at home by myself, was downright depressing. Especially when it meant time with Cooper, and a casual hangout session would be just the thing to remind me why it was so important to keep our easygoing friendship as is. "I'd be happy to help you get into trouble."

His low laugh came over the line and wrapped me in warmth. "I'll be there in a few."

. . .

Cooper and I grabbed lunch and then wandered around downtown. I asked him if he had a talk with his dad, and all he said was "Not yet."

A gold-gilded storefront with a huge window display caught my eye and I put my hand on Cooper's elbow to stop him from continuing down the sidewalk. "I know that you're a prom Scrooge, and the last thing in the world guys ever want to do is go into a store with fancy dresses, but can we go peek at the window over there?"

His hesitance was clear, but he let me pull him across the street. Four mannequins donned beautiful formals, the one in the middle shimmering in the sunshine.

Cooper heaved a sigh. "We can go in. But you're so coming with me to the sporting goods store afterward."

I let loose a squeal and gave him an attack hug before clamping on to his hand and dragging him inside.

The beautiful dresses deserved to be revered, so I hardly breathed as I approached the rows and rows of them. I walked along, occasionally lifting one up for a better view. Silk and jewel tones and slinky black and red and strappy gowns with bling, and it was totally dress heaven.

Then I saw it.

The dress.

The one I instinctually knew was destined to be mine. Gauzy beaded top, bronze sash at the waist that perfectly tied together the almost nude with a hint of gray fabric and the smoky colored tulle skirt.

I lifted the top few layers of the full, floor-length skirt. "It's so pretty. Usually I go for bright colors, so I wouldn't expect to like the combination, but this screams a night of magic under the stars. Which seems extra perfect for the *Wish Upon a Star* theme." I spun to Cooper. "Don't you think?"

He shrugged, proving that, unlike me, he had the casual gesture down pat, and making it clear his enthusiasm level for the prom hadn't grown any since we first discussed it. Not that it mattered or anything, since I was still planning on asking Mick, so I wasn't sure why that non-newsflash thought even popped into my head. "If you like it, I like it," he said.

"Do I have time to try it on?"

"Like I'm going to say no to that puppy-dog face."

Come to think of it, my lips were stuck out in a pout and I might've been batting my eyes extra, but I hadn't done it on purpose. Not that I didn't appreciate my features going to bat on my behalf, especially since it'd worked. *Please have my size, please have my size.*

My hand shook as I sorted through the hangers.

Miracle of miracles, I found my size. But I also saw the price tag. *Three hundred dollars?* "Hmm."

"What?" Cooper scooted closer.

"It's just more than I planned on spending. I haven't even asked Mick yet, either." I pinched my lip between my fingers. "Maybe I'm jumping the gun."

"It's free to try on, and the asking part's only a matter of time." Cooper put his hands on my shoulders. "Do you think I'm going to let us fail Operation Prom Date?"

"No?"

"One more time, with a little more faith."

"No." The warm fuzzies came back full force. At first I couldn't even get him to call it by name, and now he was the one giving a pep talk.

"That's right." His voice morphed into drill sergeant mode. "Now, you take that dress and you try it on."

"Yes, sir." I hugged Cooper—I couldn't seem to stop hugging him. He was super huggable, after all. The way he automatically wrapped his arms around me sent a sense of security through me that I'd never felt with a friendship before, not even when I thought Amber and I would be friends forever.

The saleswoman came over as I pulled the dress off the rack, and then she ushered me into a dressing room.

I shimmied into the dress, and I couldn't decide whether I wanted it to look amazing so I could conclude my search for the perfect dress, or if I wanted it to not fit quite right so I wouldn't justify spending that kind of money on a dress I'd only wear once.

But as the fabric fell into place and I turned to face the mirror, I decided that it'd be worth it just to feel this beautiful for one night.

Chapter Twenty-Six

COOPER

I skimmed through my phone, checking different sites as I tried not to inhale any more of the overly floral scent floating in the air of the shop. I'd shake my head at myself for getting talked into dress shopping on a Saturday, but I'd finally accepted my fate. Kate made me lose my common sense, and I was a total sucker for whatever she wanted.

The door to her dressing room swung open and I glanced up. Every ounce of oxygen left my lungs.

On the hanger, it'd just looked like a dress. On Kate, it looked… I didn't have the words. It hugged her curves and brought out her sassy side while still holding on to the sweet. I got the stars thing now, because she glittered like the night sky.

"Well?" She swooshed the skirt from side to side. "What do you think?"

Speak. Say something. Don't just stare and drool. "I think the last thing you have to worry about is not finding a date." I stood. "You look amazing."

Suddenly I understood her comment about a night of magic, too, because I was definitely under her spell.

"Thanks, Cooper." She gathered the fabric of the skirt in her hands. "I think I'll see if they'll put it on hold, and then, when I ask Mick, I'll celebrate by coming and picking it up—it'll be my reward for being brave."

Thinking of her wearing that dress at prom as she stood next to Pecker broke the spell, the slap to the face I needed to snap out of it. "Good idea." My skin itched, the need to get out of here overpowering me. "Hey, do you mind if I head over to the sporting goods store? It's just a few shops down, so you can meet me there after you've finished up here."

"Okay," she said. "I appreciate you sticking around to give me your opinion."

What she wouldn't appreciate was my real opinion, because I might not deserve her, either, but she deserved so much better than a dude who asked her guy friend if she was into hooking up.

If it wouldn't break her heart, I might tell her anyway. She was a smart girl, though. She knew what she was getting into.

I was the one who was in way over his head.

. . .

Kate frowned at her phone as I pulled up to her house.

"Something wrong?" I asked.

"I suppose it's just more the law of averages."

"Yeah, you're gonna have to translate."

Instead, she swiveled her phone to face me. Onscreen, a group of people smiled, all clad in swimwear. It took me a moment to see what had her so upset. Pecker stood front and center, and his arm was around Paris, who had on a teeny tiny bikini.

Kate's shoulders slumped. "How can I compete with that? Clearly I can't, or he would've called."

"Kate…"

She shook her head. "It's not like we're an official couple. I'm not sure why I expected…" Her chin quivered, and crying seemed inevitable, and I didn't have the slightest clue as to how to handle tears—not over Mick and some other chick. "Thanks for today. I'll see you Monday, okay?"

Before I could respond, she was out the door and up her driveway.

If she hadn't looked so devastated, I'd celebrate. I even thought of going and knocking on the door and telling her that I'd take her to prom. Oddly enough, I found the idea didn't seem so bad if it meant dancing with Kate while she was wearing that dress.

If it meant more time with Kate in general.

But I feared she'd consider it a pity date or a failure, and I wasn't sure I could deal with coming in second place.

So I decided I'd at least give her the weekend. Next time we were together, I'd try to get a better sense of how she felt about me. And if she was open to it—if she'd give me a chance—I'd show her that I could be so much better than a guy who only paid attention to her when it was convenient.

Chapter Twenty-Seven

Kate

When my phone rang on Sunday afternoon, I carefully set down the gray and navy yarn, along with the half-formed beanie. Cooper might act like knitting wasn't cool, but just wait until he had a warm hat to put on after a cold day of rowing next fall. Then he'd be thanking me.

I reached over to my nightstand and picked up my vibrating cell.

And nearly dropped it when FUTURE PROM DATE flashed across the screen. *Oh yeah. I still need to change that. Especially now, when it looks so unlikely.*

Steeling myself, I answered. "Hello?"

"What's up, sexy?" Mick asked, but before I could reply to that—or fully process his calling me sexy, because I'd probably end up asking if he'd dialed the wrong number—he added, "I think you and I should go see a movie tonight."

"Really?" It sort of slipped out, but I stood by it. He hung out with Paris yesterday, and now, what? It was my turn?

But again, we weren't dating. And technically I'd been with Cooper all day yesterday, and I'd hugged him. I'd say it was nothing more than a friendly gesture, but the way my heart skipped as I remembered it told a different story.

"Um. Yeah. Yesterday I was at the lake with a group of friends, so I missed your call. I was hoping we could hang out tonight, though. Just you and me. I'll even let you pick the movie."

His story about being at the lake with a group of friends matched up with the picture I'd seen. The image popped into my head again, because okay, I might've looked at it more than once yesterday after Cooper dropped me off. It seemed like proof of my failure to snag Mick, but I supposed if I took a more objective approach, a picture of his arm around another girl wasn't exactly a smoking gun. He didn't have his lips on Paris's, at least, but I couldn't help wanting to know if they had been at any point in the afternoon.

Demanding more facts would definitely not come across as casual and cool. And say he and Paris did…kiss or whatever. He wanted to take me out tonight on a real date, not just drag me along to a group hangout. That was progress, and could transition nicely to prom. "Okay. Let's go to a movie. But I'm holding you to letting me pick."

We went over details, said our good-byes, and I hung up the phone—before saying anything stupid, no less.

I resumed my knitting, pausing to turn up my show so I could hear the dialogue over the light clacking noise of the needles, and smiled as I thought about my upcoming date.

Mick never should've given me free reign to choose the movie, because I was getting a little sick of compromises. Tonight, he'd have to make one.

With that goal in mind, I balanced my yarn and needles in one hand, tapped my phone to pull up movie times, and looked for the girliest, most romantic movie out there.

• • •

Mick didn't flinch when I told him I wanted to watch the romantic comedy.

The scent of movie popcorn overpowered me as we walked through the lobby—I suspected they piped the scent into the air vents, too, in the name of sales. Mick bought a bucket, asked what candy and soda I liked, and bought me those as well.

Armed with a giant Dr Pepper and sour gummi worms, we made our way into the dim theater. Mick told me to pick wherever I wanted, and I made my way to a fairly empty spot in the middle of the rows.

By the time the previews started, I was having a harder and harder time convincing myself to stay detached and cautious. I'd put a lot of time and effort into my crush, and now I got to sit right next to him and enjoy his chiseled features doing their perfect thing up close.

Yet I ate my candy, using it almost as a shield so he couldn't grab my hand, whereas when this entire operation started, I would've needed it more to keep my hands busy because of nerves.

But that's because I'm getting more comfortable around him, which is good.

Halfway through the movie, he moved my empty soda cup to the other side of him and lifted the armrest between us. Then he wrapped his arm around my shoulders and curled me close.

One Month Ago Me would've died and gone to heaven. And it wasn't that I didn't enjoy snuggling with Mick—the soapy fresh scent meant he'd showered recently, and I could feel the muscles in his arm flex every time he moved. There was certainly nothing wrong with the muscles in his chest, either.

I couldn't pinpoint exactly why my excitement hadn't

reached levels of epic proportions until the drive away from the movie theater. He was in the middle of giving me a blow-by-blow of his last game of the season—for the record, I'd asked, but I didn't expect him to be so detailed. I figured he'd say it was awesome, not speak in foreign terms that made me think *This is what Cooper deals with when I discuss my fandoms, only I'm pretty sure I explain better and at least add in a little extra flair to make it more entertaining.*

And there it was. The thing holding me back from fully jumping in and squeeing like a girl at ComicCon who'd just met her favorite actor.

Instead of enjoying Mick's cocky smirk, I missed Cooper's easy, dimpled smile. Missed the ability to make random comments about fictional couples with smooshed together names and know that while he didn't totally get my fandoms, he liked that side of me. I longed for the scent of his woodsy cologne, and the teasing, and the sense of security.

Ugh, I was about to mess everything up for a guy who only thought of me as a friend. A guy who'd actually balked when I'd asked him to touch my knee for a joke. In fact, almost every time he touched me, he jerked away like my skin had burned him.

Except for hugs—he ruled at hugs and seemed to be good with those.

Friends hug.

Occasionally we hold hands… Usually it's more of a supportive gesture, one I need…

If he liked me as more than a friend, there was no way he'd be doing so much to help me land Mick. That was as much proof as I needed right there.

"…my house?" Mick asked.

My mind tried to replay his question, as if I had that sort of power. "I'm sorry. What about your house?"

"I asked if you wanted me drop you off, or if you could

hang for a while at my house."

I bit my lip. His gaze dropped to my mouth, and he swallowed, that kind of swallow guys did in the movies when they were thinking about the girl in a more-than-friends way. Did I really affect him like that? Did he expect more than kissing at his house?

"With school tomorrow, my mom expects me home," I said, a strange mix of relief and disappointment going through me that I couldn't simply let go and see what happened if I went home with him. "Maybe we could hang out at your house some other time?"

"Of course. You could come over after school tomorrow."

"I'm supposed to go rowing with Cooper. I'm helping him train." *And with the Spring Festival race less than two weeks away, he'll want to hit it hard, no doubt.*

Mick reached across the console of the car and took my hand. He lifted it to his lips and kissed the back of it. "Maybe you could skip a day?"

A tingle worked its way across my skin. See? There was something there. I was just overanalyzing as usual, psyching myself out. "I'll see what I can do."

His signature smirk spread across his mouth.

"So, you said you were hanging out at the lake yesterday," I said as he turned down my street. "Do you do that often?" I was fishing for information. So sue me. I didn't want to make a fool of myself by asking him to prom, and the more intel I had, the better.

Of course he probably wouldn't tell me if he had a date unless I brought it up. And I wanted to add that I'd seen a picture so my question didn't seem so random, but then that'd make me look psycho, and I figured random was the better option.

"Now and then. Paris asked me to go, but honestly, the entire time, I couldn't stop wishing you were there." He pulled up in front of my house and put his car in park. His eyes met mine. "More and more I find myself thinking about you. There's something about you, Kate. I can't get you out of my head."

Stuttered breaths fell from my lips, one after another, leaving me dizzy. "I've, uh, been thinking about you more and more, too." Truthfully, I'd been thinking about him less than I used to, but I'm sure that was just because I was super busy.

He leaned closer, and thoughts about the many girls he'd kissed swirled through my brain, pushing my stupid insecurity about not measuring up to the forefront. If I sucked at kissing, would he still go with me to prom?

So I gave him the quickest peck ever, more an ambush than a kiss, and reached for my door handle. "My mom's watching out the window. But, uh, see you tomorrow? And thanks for the movie and the snacks and everything."

His mouth hung open, and the way he blinked at me made me think no other girl had left him hanging like that.

I'm so, so stupid. Why couldn't I just kiss him? I blew it. I blew it, and now I'm not going to get to wear that pretty dress I put on hold.

I slammed the car door and rushed up the sidewalk to my house. Once I was inside, I leaned against my door and bumped my head against it a couple times.

My dream bubble bounced out of reach, headed toward sharp rocks that'd pop it for sure.

I'd already put half down on that amazing formal gown, money I couldn't get back. But I didn't want it back. I wanted to wear the dress. I didn't want to wear it on a pity date, either. Senior prom was my last big high school event, and after a pretty meh experience, I wanted one night of big, dramatic romance, even if it took fancy expensive dresses and decorations to facilitate it.

I spotted Mom's keys hanging next to the door—her friend Nadine had picked her up earlier for some dinner party they were going to. I had permission to drive the car in emergencies, and this was definitely an emergency.

After a quick check to make sure Mick's vehicle was gone, I climbed into the car and took off, hoping a drive would help me untangle my thoughts.

Earlier I'd let my overly analytical side get in my way. My anxiety had mixed in with the thoughts of failure I experienced yesterday, and I'd gotten all confused and turned around. Friends were the people you were most comfortable with, so *of course* being around Cooper was easier than being on a date with the guy I'd crushed on forever and dreamed of taking to prom.

I couldn't let my dream go without a fight. I'd let too much pass me by. I'd put so much time into it, too. I thought about the missions Dad and I used to do. We'd never failed one, not even when the package with Mom's funky Scooby Doo salt and pepper shakers got hung up in Springfield, Massachusetts. We'd hopped in the car and driven two hours each way through a rainstorm so she'd have them on her birthday, not the day after.

The entire time Dad grumbled about how fast he could've flown there, while I gripped the handle over the window thinking we practically *were* flying.

No rainstorm stood in my way; no significant amount of miles. Nope, the only thing in my way now was me, and I wasn't about to fail a mission now.

I had to do something to fix how awkward I'd been at the end of that date, and I needed to do it now, before I lost my nerve.

Even if it was drastic.

Even if it tested every boundary.

I scrolled through my contacts, found the one I was looking for, and called the number. "Can you meet me at the lake?" I asked as soon as he picked up.

"I'll be right there."

Chapter Twenty-Eight

I paced the dock near my house, the wood creaking underneath my feet. The stars shone brightly through the cloudless sky, but I couldn't concentrate on constellations right now.

Headlights cut through the dark, growing brighter and brighter, and I lifted a hand to shield my eyes. Dust swirled around the SUV as it came to a stop, and then Kate climbed out.

My heart caught, and it took every ounce of my willpower to not run over to her. After all, there could be a hundred reasons she needed to meet, and most likely none of them were the one I wanted. The one where she realized she was as crazy about me as I was her, and we could forget Pecker and the Operation and everyone else.

"I know it's late," she said as she approached. Dark gray eye shadow covered her lids, she had on pale pink lipstick, and her lacy white top exposed one shoulder, adding to the sweet yet not-that-sweet look that drove me crazy.

"It's okay."

She twisted one of her curls around her finger, frantic energy radiating off her in waves. "Did I wake you up? You sounded like I might've woken you up."

I put my hands on her shoulders and looked her in the eyes. "Kate. I'm here now. What's going on?"

"It's really embarrassing, and now I'm re-thinking it, and…" She glanced away. "It's going to sound crazy…" She bit her lip, and my eyes focused there. "But then again…"

Her jitteriness transferred to me, stretching my nerves tight. I lifted one hand from her shoulder and cupped her chin, twisting her face back toward mine. "You know I'm here for you—no matter what it is. But I can't help if you don't tell me what's going on."

"Tonight Mick took me to the movies. Then afterward, we were in his car, and… I can't believe I'm going to tell you this…"

Ice coursed through my veins. If she talked about hooking up with Pecker, I was going to break something. His face might be a nice thing to start with.

"The last few times I've hung out with Mick, I've been sure that he's going to kiss me… He leans in, and our lips will be so close to touching…"

Torture. Salt-on-an-open wound, burning, slicing torture.

"And I just freeze," she said. "He senses it, because how could he not, and then things get awkward. Tonight I, like, slam kissed him. Even though our lips technically touched, it wasn't even really a kiss. I freaked and bolted out of his truck as fast as I could." That crinkle showed up in her forehead and her lips pressed into a tight line. "I think I blew it. I don't think he'll ever talk to me again—not unless I make the next move, and it's got to be big."

I sucked in a deep breath and slowly let it out. "Oh-kay."

"Part of the problem is I get all psyched out because I start thinking about how many girls he's kissed, and I only ever kissed one other boy, and it was horrible."

"You've only kissed one guy?" I blurted out without thinking, but seriously, how could only one guy have kissed her? I'd wanted to kiss her from pretty much the first moment we started hanging out together.

"Yes, but focus on the right part. It was *horrible*. Not anything like the movies or TV shows, and I was so disappointed my first kiss was so dreadful. And I thought it was him—like he was all open mouth, fish lips coming at me. But lately, I wonder if it wasn't me. Maybe I suck at kissing."

Oxygen rushed into my lungs, but no air came out, they just inflated and inflated, to the point of being painful. As hard as I tried not to look at her lips again, my traitorous eyes dipped, and longing lanced my heart.

"See?" She curled her arms around herself. "You're not saying anything, which means you know I'm right."

"That's not why I'm not saying anything. I don't know what to say, but I know that you don't suck at kissing."

"How could you know that?"

"I just do," I said, and I accidentally leaned closer, like her lips were magnetic and calling for me to test them out.

"I almost looked up tips the other night, but even the thought of it is mortifying…" Her cheeks blushed an adorable pink. "There is one other option I thought of." She swallowed hard and looped a finger through her necklace, sending that hypnotizing charm in the center of it swinging back and forth. "I thought maybe, if I had someone teach me…? Someone I trusted…?"

Her words clicked into place. The way she looked at me, with a mix of pleading and worry, solidified it. She wanted me to teach her to kiss.

Talk about line crossing.

But I wasn't sure I was strong enough to refuse, and for once, it had nothing to do with trying to help her out.

Chapter Twenty-Nine

As soon as the words left my mouth I wanted to stuff them back in. Yet I couldn't take it back. I needed help, and Cooper had been with me through this entire journey. The fact I'd made it so far only proved he knew what he was doing.

The longer he stared, the tighter my skin stretched, and my heart ceased working correctly, doing a thudding instead of beating thing in my chest.

Then the hand he had on my shoulder slowly drifted up and cupped my neck, his thumb resting against the pulse point underneath my jaw.

My blood rushed there in response, so quickly it left me dizzy.

"It's really pretty simple," he said, but his voice was huskier than usual. He lowered his head, his mouth lined up with mine.

I reached up and curled my hand around his forearm, sure I was going to need to hold on to something.

"Ready?" he whispered, his breath hitting my lips.

My voice didn't work, so I nodded.

His gaze bored into me for one long, intense second, and then he pressed his lips to mine. A thrill shot through me, from where our mouths made contact all the way down to my toes.

He increased the pressure, teasing my lips farther apart. His arm wound around my waist, and he used it to pull me tighter to him. I melted into his embrace and captured his bottom lip between both of mine.

I sucked it lightly, euphoria tingling through me when he groaned.

His tongue swept into my mouth, just a brief taste that set my body on fire.

Oh yeah, this *is what kissing is supposed to be like.*

I drove my fingers through his hair and he tilted his head, deepening the kiss and leaving the world spinning around us.

Time froze and sped up.

The ground fell out from under me.

And I wanted more.

I tipped onto my toes and ran my tongue across his lips. His fingers dug into my skin as he eradicated every inch of space between us, and when he swirled his tongue around mine, I was grateful for my grip on his arm and his strong hold on me, because my knees buckled.

But he didn't let me fall.

He never let me fall.

When we broke apart, he looked at me, his eyes dazed. But as soon as he blinked, they sharpened and he cleared his throat. "So, yeah. Something like that."

I raised a hand and pressed my fingertips to my still tingling lips. I didn't know what to say. I wasn't sure I was capable of speech anymore. Breathing pretty much took all my effort right now, and the world hadn't stopped spinning yet.

Finally I found my voice. "Um, well…thanks. Coach." Now I sort of wished my voice had stayed lost. Since I couldn't stop the awkward train once it was in motion, I even added a punch to his shoulder.

Cooper's eyebrows drew together. He ran a hand through his hair and glanced back at his house. "Guess I better get back before my parents realize I'm gone."

But the sparks! I needed to know if he felt the sparks, too. They were still shooting through me, laying waste to every tingle and flutter I'd ever felt with Mick, and making me crave more.

Say something…

"I should probably get home, too."

Not that. But here I was thinking about our kiss, and he seemed to be looking to escape. If he wanted more—if he'd felt the sparks I had—this was the perfect opportunity for him to say so.

Then again, I supposed *I* could say something. Maybe. I licked my lips, my heart pumping double time, but fear held me back—fear of rejection and of messing up our friendship, and I couldn't stop thinking about those awful days where he'd needed space, and how hard it would be to get through the rest of the school year without him. "See you tomorrow?"

"Yeah," he said, his gaze skimming right over me. "Tomorrow."

A tight band formed around my chest, and I scolded myself for letting my emotions get tangled up in his kissing lesson. *I should've known this was a horrible idea.* Honestly, I hadn't been thinking clearly at all, and that was the problem. Impulsive emotional decisions never worked out well for me. Carefully laid plans with bullet points were where it was at.

Cooper started away, and my heart dropped to my toes. Then he spun back and gave me a half smile that held a hint of sorrow. "'Night, Kate. I hope all your dreams come true."

Which meant that he wanted me to take Mick to prom, right?

I didn't even wish him a good night. I just stood there, beyond confused, wondering when I'd let myself fall for the wrong boy.

Chapter Thirty

KATE

Armed with the knowledge of how to kiss, I approached Mick in the school hallway, telling myself to ignore the people around him.

But at the last minute I chickened out and dodged the other way.

Actually, calling it chickening out was chickening out in its own way. My detour was more about thinking about someone else than being scared to talk to Mick. I was too afraid to dive deep into that complication, though, because I wasn't sure how the other half of that equation felt about me.

On my way to my locker, several guys smiled at me—including one of Mick's closest friends, which I thought was weird. Did that mean Mick didn't tell them we'd gone on a date?

A few girls whispered, and I swore it was about me, because I got fake, snide smiles when I passed them. *What's going on? Did I enter some kind of alternate universe?*

Chalking it up to not getting any sleep last night—I'd relived my kiss with Cooper countless times, tossing and turning as I thought about how I wanted to do it again, and how crossing that line would be a huge risk to our friendship, so it couldn't happen again. Then I tossed some more as I replayed how unaffected he'd seemed—to the point that I wondered if he was lying when he told me I could kiss.

Frustration and confusion now mixing in with the twilight zone feeling, I grabbed my books and headed toward my morning classes.

My heart sped up when I spotted Cooper in the crowd.

I didn't know if I should let my thoughts wander to where they were going, but it was too late to stop them anyway. They dwelled on the delicious sensations the press of Cooper's lips brought on. The way he wrapped his arm around my waist and held me so tightly to him. The touch of his tongue to mine.

Residual heat coursed through me, the frenzied butterflies in my gut now gliding around with wings on fire.

Maybe… Maybe it could *happen again.*

Afterward he'd been closed off, but during that kiss, he'd been anything but. His low groan, the way his fingers dug into my sides—that wasn't unaffected behavior. Right?

I suppose after Amber, I stopped trying a bit. Maybe even retreated into myself. Putting myself out there was hard, and the sting of rejection hadn't faded as much as I wished it would. It made it hard to take another chance, especially one with such high stakes attached—the statistician in me couldn't help calculating the odds, and when it came to Cooper, even a one percent chance of messing things up between us didn't seem worth it.

In a lot of ways, Mick was the safer option. While I'd had a crush on him for a long time, it was all attraction and daydream based, so my heart wasn't all caught up in him, completely exposed and unprotected.

If Cooper rejected me, on the other hand, I didn't know if I would ever get over it. It'd be like Amber ditching me times a thousand. I'd experience that crushing loss that sucked away happiness and accentuated loneliness, and just the thought was enough to give me heart palpitations with a squeezing side of anxiety.

Arms wound around my waist, and I thought Cooper must've seen me having a panic attack and come to steady me.

Instead, Mick's voice filled my ear as my back met his chest. "Morning, sexy."

Disappointment flooded me, and I worked to wipe it off my face before I spun around. "Morning. I'm, um, kind of—"

"In a rush? As usual?"

I smiled. "Yeah, actually."

Mick hooked his finger in my belt loop. "Even though that flick was super cheesy, I had a good time at the movies last night."

"Uh, yeah. Me, too." I decided not to mention I thought the movie was romantic and swoony, not cheesy, because that conversation would take too much time and my thoughts were too tangled up with other swoony romantic sensations I'd experienced last night near the shore of the lake. "Can I talk to you at lunch? Like I said, in a rush."

"Actually, I said it for you, because you're always rushing off in the mornings." Mick tapped my nose, and it was a cute gesture and all, but I wasn't feeling it. Everything felt off, and I supposed that was the push I needed.

"Okay, well, see you later." I broke away and sprinted down the hall, past worrying if it made me look like a crazy person—I didn't give a damn about looking too serious anymore, either.

I caught up to Cooper right before he turned into the English department hallway, which was in the opposite wing of my first class. I was working on not worrying my impulsive move might make me late, because I needed to see where he and I were at before I made any more decisions.

My tightening throat made speaking suddenly seem impossible, but this was Cooper, so I forced myself to push through my nerves. "Hey."

Okay, so it wasn't, like, a lot of words, or a grand declaration or anything, but seriously, why were my hands shaking?

He barely glanced at me. "Hey. I'm kind of in a hurry."

Ironic, considering I'd just blown off Mick with the same excuse, which wasn't helping with the shaking hands thing. I grabbed Cooper's arm and pulled him to a stop, my pulse thundering in my ears. "I understand hurries and not wanting to be late for class and all, but I…" *Need a sign that I'm not alone in thinking that we're great together.*

For you to look at me or talk to me at the very least.

When I didn't get any of those things, I cleared my throat. "I just wanted to say thanks again. For last night."

I held my breath as hope and desire flooded my chest, waiting to see if I saw a spark. Saw that he couldn't stop thinking about our kiss, either. Something. *Anything.*

Standing there, my hand on his arm, it hit me, so strongly my knees wobbled. I didn't want someone who made me incapable of speech. I wanted someone who I could talk with about my passions and hobbies and anything and everything. Someone who made me laugh, who truly knew me, and made me feel completely unsteady in the best possible way.

I didn't want safe and risk free. I wanted the boy who kissed me under the starlit sky last night.

I wanted Cooper Callihan.

He didn't even look at me. "Sure thing."

My heart dropped to the floor, taking my hope along with it. I pinched the charm of my necklace between my fingers. "I'm afraid I crossed a line, and I worried—"

"It's fine, Kate. What are friends for?"

The word *friends* shouldn't have stabbed me in the chest the way it did. I needed his friendship. He was my only friend. *Of course* he had only been trying to help me last night.

"Like I said, I'm in a hurry. I'll catch you later." Without waiting for me to respond, he quickened his pace and charged down the hall.

I blinked back tears. *Get it together.* Blaming lack of sleep for being overly emotional—might as well blame it for everything—I rushed to my first class of the day, where I focused on the material like I'd never focused before.

At lunch, Mick strolled up to me and draped an arm around my neck, his hand dangling dangerously close to my right breast. "Are you off the hook for this afternoon?"

I gripped the cardboard box with my lunch inside tighter so I wouldn't drop it. "Off the hook?"

Vaguely I noticed he'd walked us over to the table with his friends. "With Callihan?" Mick's eyebrows arched up. "And the rowing thing?" His look turned from questioning to frustration. "Didn't you say you were going to try to get out of training with him so you could hang with me instead?"

"Oh. Right. I'll talk to him." *Not that he'll talk back. He'll probably be in too big of a hurry.*

"She'll do more than talk to him," Paris muttered from her seat to our left. "I have to give it to you, Kate. I never thought you'd be the type of girl to juggle all the guys."

I stiffened. Then I dared a glance at Mick. "I'm not…" Hell, maybe I accidentally was. But one thing was for sure: I definitely wasn't doing a good job.

"Back off, Paris," he said. "Jealousy doesn't look good on you."

Her mouth dropped open and she spun toward her group of friends with a huff. Amber eyed me, looking like she didn't recognize me—which seemed a bit like the pot calling the kettle black, but whatever.

I wanted to run, but I sat down instead. If Cooper didn't like me as more than a friend, I couldn't blow everything with Mick right now. Surely a bit more time with him, and my feelings for Cooper would fade.

My gaze automatically sought him out, obviously not getting the memo about us trying not to think about Cooper right now. He and Jaden sat at their usual spot with Alana. A studious guy was next to her, his lips moving a hundred miles a minute. He didn't seem to notice everyone else looked bored out of their minds.

Despite whatever drab topic the dude was going on and on about, longing to be sitting over there and listening in rose, giving me a torn-apart sensation.

Cooper slumped back and scanned the room.

Our eyes caught, and he gave me a big thumbs-up. Actual encouragement over sitting next to Mick, and it should feel like a win.

But it didn't.

When I dragged my attention off Cooper, Mick gave me an inquisitive look. Right. I needed to be putting in my time here, finishing up my mission so I could put on my fancy expensive dress and go to prom with a guy who *wanted* to kiss me instead of one who dealt with doing so in the name of friendship.

"About what Paris said…" I didn't even know how to finish that up, but I felt like I needed to explain before he got the wrong idea—the idea everyone else apparently had about me now.

"It's not a big deal. Callihan told me that you weren't into serious."

A sinking sensation went through my gut. "He did?" Our plan included me coming across that way, sure, but he'd actually told Mick that? I thought we were more about show than tell. Telling was different, and more…just *more*. My trust felt completely violated, and the raw feeling in my chest that'd started somewhere around the strained conversation with Cooper in the hall this morning grew even wider.

"Yeah. I don't want to be tied down right now, either. It's stupid to start anything when school's almost over and we'll just be heading to college soon."

"Right. That's exactly how I feel." My voice came out scratchy, the lie shredding it on the way out. How had I ended up here?

Oh yeah. I set a goal and decided I'd do whatever it took to achieve it. I lifted my sandwich and forced myself to take a bite, even though I no longer felt very hungry. "So that wouldn't bother you? If he and I were…?"

"Only if you blow me off for him this afternoon." Mick moved his lips next to my ear as his hand curled around my thigh. "I have plans, and they involve me and you, alone in my house."

Man, if Mick's friends thought I was a hookup girl, no wonder they were extra friendly. An icky feeling settled in my gut, turning my one bite of food sour. This wasn't how I wanted to end my high school years—being known as the girl who went from shy and serious to not shy or serious at all. Maybe other girls were okay being that kind of girl, but it wasn't me, and honestly, I was sick of working so hard to be someone I wasn't.

I've certainly landed myself in a mess this time. Worse, I had no idea how to get myself out of it.

It needed to be by myself, too, because clearly I had to do the rest of this mission *without* Cooper Callihan.

Chapter Thirty-One

Kissing Kate had been a mistake. Not because it wasn't amazing, because it *was*. I couldn't stop thinking about it, and I wanted to do it again and again and never stop kissing her. But the stabbing jealousy I experienced every time I saw her with Mick made it hard to breathe or think, slicing so much deeper now that I knew what her soft lips felt like against mine. How it felt to hold her in my arms and have her cling to me as if she never planned on letting go.

For a few amazing minutes last night, I'd convinced myself she felt the same way I did, because otherwise the kiss wouldn't have overpowered me like that. But when I saw her in the hallway with Mick first thing this morning, his arms around her as he whispered in her ear, reality came crashing in. I was the guinea pig guy. Practice for the real thing.

When it came to deciding exactly what *I* wanted to do with my life, I struggled to make a solid decision. Partially because Dad already made it for me, but honestly, committing to one thing for the rest of my life made my chest squeeze too tight. It seemed so final, and with most of my life stretched in front of me, I didn't want to choose wrong and end up living with regrets. The only thing I'd ever fully committed to was rowing, which had to do with my love for gliding through the water more than team spirit.

For the first time in my life, I was completely sure of one thing I wanted, no second-guessing, no fear over thinking in long-term scenarios.

I wanted Kate.

I wanted her sitting next to me in the cab of my truck, or in my boat, or on the foot of my bed—or really, wherever, because it didn't matter where we were when I was with her. I wanted to listen to her babble on and on about couples she shipped in that dreamy yet passionate tone, and to show her constellations as we laid out under the stars and laughed and talked until both of us were too hoarse to speak. Then we'd speak in other ways, kissing until her breaths were mine, and mine were hers.

I'd tried not to hope—even shut my emotions off the best I could the instant the kiss ended—but after a night of tossing and turning, I'd decided I was going to tell her how I felt. With my attraction moving into the consuming range, simply avoiding her wasn't going to be enough to repress it, and I knew I couldn't hold back how I felt anymore.

Or that was what I thought before I saw her with *him*.

I'd detached myself the best I could this morning so I wouldn't explode when she'd tried to talk to me—no doubt about how successful kissing practice had been at helping her be more comfortable with Mick. I'd felt so ripped open and raw, I couldn't even look at her. I kept telling myself I couldn't get mad at her when she'd been crystal clear about the point of our deal and I was the sucker who went along with it, but I was angry all the same.

Then she was with him at lunch, too, which only rubbed salt in the wound, and I'd had a pointless day of classes where I couldn't focus for shit.

Stupid me, I'd still kept an iron grip on that tiny glimmer of hope that called to me and said once we were alone in my boat, I could do something to make her see me and how amazing we could be together, and get her to change her mind. Get her to pick me instead.

While staring at the door of the school, holding my breath as I waited for her to come out, my phone had chimed with a text from her.

Then it became painfully clear I needed to face the fact that she didn't want me the way I did her.

I'd lost her, but even worse, she hadn't ever been mine.

I looked down and re-read the text.

Kate: *I know this is totally hypocritical of me, but I can't meet you for rowing practice today. I need some space.*

Yeah, space from me so you can get with Mick. I'd mildly disliked the guy before, but that'd just been upgraded to loathing with a fiery passion.

I climbed in my truck, slamming the door shut, and peeled out of the school parking lot. The lake would only make me think of Kate, so I went home to wallow.

The second I stepped into the living room, I kicked myself for not going to the lake. Or at least checking the garage before coming inside.

Dad sat at the table, dozens of legal documents spread out in front of him. He looked at me before I could attempt to dart up the stairs unnoticed. "Hey, son. I just got this new case. You should come take a look. Get a taste for the files you'll be digging into this summer."

I moved over to him and the words on the multiple files

blurred together. Evidently knowing what I wanted with Kate—even though I couldn't have it—unlocked the part of me where all my desires lay, and they wanted to burst out and make themselves known. I'd already had it with today, and I figured it couldn't get much worse.

I cleared my throat and looked at my father. "I don't want to be a lawyer. I want to be on the rowing team and study marine biology. I'll probably minor in astronomy while I'm at it."

"If rowing's that important to you, you can be on the team. But that's not a good bachelor's degree to help you get into law school. And they certainly won't be impressed by astronomy as a minor."

Frustration bubbled up inside me, threatening to burst free, but I knew yelling would only drive this conversation into explosive territory. "Well, if you listened to the first part of that statement, I don't want to be a lawyer, so going to law school would be a waste of time."

Dad's eyes lifted to mine, anger simmering in the brown. "I know it's a lot of school. But Callihan men are lawyers. It's in our blood. Hasn't it provided a nice life for you? My work is what allows you to be out goofing around on that lake all the time."

I ignored the goofing around jab, still trying to keep our discussion civil. "I appreciate all you've done for me, I do. But that doesn't mean I'm going to live the rest of my life working a job I don't want."

Dad rose and leaned over the table, his posture all intimidation. "If you think I'm going to pay your tuition so you can go dink around, you're wrong."

I straightened and looked him square in the face. "Then I guess you'll have to get used to the idea of your only son going to community college."

A muscle flexed his jaw and he narrowed his eyes. "Where

is this coming from? Is it that girl you've been hanging out with? Your mom says you two are close—don't tell me you're going to give up college to be with your high school girlfriend." His tone made it clear how laughable and pathetic that'd be.

Steel filled my lungs, leaving them too heavy. "If Kate was my girlfriend, I just might. But she'd never ask me to give up what I wanted to do—she'd encourage me to go for my dreams. The truth is, I've felt this way for a long time. I didn't want to disappoint you, or to make you mad enough to lose your temper." I threw up a hand. "Mom and I tiptoe around you, trying to make sure there's no noise and no mess here to keep you happy. But I can't live like that forever. More than that, I shouldn't have to. And neither should Mom."

Red flooded his face, his anger reaching the boiling point. "If you think I'm just going to let you throw away your life—"

"Paul." Mom stepped into the room. "Can you just listen to him? Listen to what he's saying. Just for once, *listen*."

"You've babied him too much," Dad shot at Mom before pointing his finger in my face. "You're doing the summer internship, and you're getting your law degree. End of story. Now, it looks like I'm going to have to take this to the office instead of spending a quiet night here like I hoped to." He swept his files off the table and tucked them under one arm. "I hope you're both happy."

With that, he stormed out of the room. The slam of his office door echoed through the hall.

I ran a hand through my hair and let out an exhale. "That went well."

"He'll calm down, and then hopefully he'll be more open to a rational conversation," Mom said, moving over to me.

"We're talking about the same guy, right? He's going to come up with three hundred arguments to prove his side, and there's nothing you or I can say to change his mind. I appreciate the support, but you should just save yourself his anger and agree with him next time." I turned to walk out of the room, but Mom stopped me with a hand on my shoulder.

"If you can be brave, so can I. We can't tiptoe around him all the time. One day he's going to have to learn that having a family means there will be people who live here and make noise, and occasionally even messes."

I shook my head. "I'm not brave."

If I were, I would've told Kate how I really felt, despite having the odds stacked against me. I wouldn't just let her go to prom with some idiot who didn't even know what a lucky bastard he was.

• • •

"Cooper?"

I spun around to find Amber. Since she and I had barely exchanged words this year, I fought the urge to scratch my head over her sudden appearance at my locker. The anxious body language confused me even more. "Yeah?"

"Do you have a date for the prom?"

"I'm not going to prom," I said.

She glanced down at her feet. "But if someone asked, maybe you'd change your mind?"

"Who? Paris? Whatever mild flirtation she and I had ended long ago."

Amber frowned. "I don't do everything for Paris. I'm asking for me. I hoped you'd go to prom with me. I figured since Kate's going with Mick…"

My stomach bottomed out. "She asked him?"

"I'm not sure who asked who. I just heard that they're going together." She leaned in and whispered, "Paris is super pissed about it." If I wasn't mistaken, Amber looked a little gleeful over her supposed friend's anger.

But I couldn't concentrate too much on that, because all I

could think about was Mick and Kate. *She asked him to prom. It's really over.*

I didn't think I had any hope left, but the gut-punch, heart-clench combo made it clear I'd been holding on to something, and it'd just been ripped from me and squashed like a bug.

Kate and Mick. At prom. He'd push for more than kissing on a night like that, and I wanted to do something to stop it, but it wasn't my place, and she'd made her decision.

I hated her decision.

It'd be torture to be there and see them together.

"So? What do you say?" Amber flashed me a big smile. "Will you be my date for prom?"

Chapter Thirty-Two

I will not cry, I will not cry, I will not cry...

Glittery streamers surrounded me, dammit. Not to mention the shimmery gossamer. The decorations the prom committee ordered came in today, so we were sorting them and checking to see we had everything. But I couldn't concentrate on the pretty decorations, or what my dress would look like next to them, because I'd just overheard Paris talking to Minion #1 about how Amber had asked Cooper to prom.

And he'd said yes.

The image I'd had of him in a tux by my side evaporated for good, and I regretted not asking him to go with me, even as just friends. Every pump of my heart spread the misery flooding my chest farther, making it that much harder not to give in to the urge to cry.

While Cooper acted like he hated all things prom, Amber was super pretty, and that no doubt factored heavily into his decision to go with her to the dance he was suddenly okay with attending.

I'm sure he didn't waste a second before saying yes.

The guy I now needed to ask by default? Not so much on the surety scale. He'd tried to kiss me yesterday at his house. I'd pulled back, and that time it had nothing to do with freezing up or thinking about how many other girls he'd kissed.

It had to do with the fact that I couldn't stop thinking about the cute rower who'd given me kissing lessons under the stars. If those were novice lessons, I definitely wanted to get to the super advanced level—I was all about practice making perfect with Cooper's lips, even if our kiss had been so amazing I didn't know how it could possibly get any more perfect.

Mick had been gentlemanly enough about the entire situation. I told him that I was sorry, but I moved slower than he was used to, and while he looked completely befuddled—probably because Cooper implied I just hooked up with guys all the freaking time, which still ate at me—he politely drove me home.

He didn't talk to me at lunch, though.

Not that I talked to him, either.

I ran into Jaden as I'd been holding my lunch, unable to commit to either side of the cafeteria, and he'd asked, "Trouble in paradise?"

"With me and...Cooper, you mean?" If Cooper had mentioned the tension and weirdness between us to Jaden, then maybe I wasn't all alone on Sappy Island, missing him while he didn't think twice about me.

"Oh no," Jaden said. "I know you guys are just friends. Cooper told me you had a thing for Mick Pecker. But just know that you're welcome at our table any time."

Anger had coursed through me, every ounce of confidence I'd gathered the past month melted, and I'd left the cafeteria without talking to anyone else. How dare Cooper tell people about my crush on Mick! What part of top-secret mission was so hard to understand? Who else knew? If Mick found out the level of my obsession he'd run screaming.

For all I knew, he already wanted to.

More and more, Operation Prom Date looked to be a total bust. Maybe I'd sit at home in my beautiful formal gown and re-watch *Arrow* episodes while mainlining soda and cookie dough. At least the dress would see some action, even if it were onscreen and involved way more fighting than kissing.

When the kissing did happen on that show, though... Tears blurred my eyes, the packing list in my hands swimming in two. If not even Olicity could cheer me up, then I was utterly and totally screwed.

The more I thought about it, the more tears pressed on my eyes. Before I made a fool of myself and made Paris's day by giving her enough emotional ammo to scar me for life, I dropped the checklist on the pile of decorations and rushed out of the room.

And slammed right into Cooper.

His hands came up on my waist as he steadied me, and the intense desire that automatically flared to life was torture. Like the type of torture where shows flashed-forward and expected you to be cool with the canon couples suddenly not being together anymore.

I blinked away my tears as quickly as he wanted me to row, desperate to stop them. "*Ugh*, of course *you're* here."

Cooper's expression hardened. "I see how it is. Once you've gotten what you want, you throw away the person who helped you."

"Were you helping when you told Mick I was a hookup girl? Or when you told Jaden I had a thing for Mick? Was anything we did kept secret?" My voice cracked, so I put more force behind it, making sure it was as sharp as the pain in my chest. "Or did you tell everyone about how pathetic I am, that I needed help to land a prom date?"

Cooper grabbed my arm and pulled me away from the crowd of people who were starting to stare. "Look, I didn't say anything to anyone, except for telling Jaden that you liked

Mick, so not to bother wasting his time with you. But you're about to tell everyone yourself. *Jeez.*"

Defeat weighed me down, along with a good dose of sorrow that Cooper and I couldn't even be civil to each other anymore. That wasted time comment hurt like hell, too, sending the pain deeper, until even my bones ached with it. I clenched my jaw, renewing my chant of *I will not cry, I will not cry.* "What does it matter anymore, anyway? Might as well just let everyone know. Maybe if I tell them first I'll at least sound a little less desperate."

"I don't understand why *you* get to be mad," Cooper said. "You got what you wanted. You're going to prom with Pecker. If anyone should be mad, it's me. You bailed on our rowing sessions, leaving me in the lurch. And let's not forget how you convinced me to talk to my dad. It went horrible, by the way, and then were you there, like you promised you'd be?"

My beat-up heart splatted in my chest. How could I be there when being around him only made me think about what I'd never have? Still, he was right. I'd sent the message about needing space, copping out when I should've been there for him. "I'm sorry. He freaked out? Are you okay?"

Cooper made a disgusted noise in the back of his throat. "Don't act like you care now."

"I do care!"

Mick came over and put his hand on my back. He narrowed his eyes at Cooper. "Is everything okay here?"

"Great. Of course it's you." Cooper shook his head. "This is just perfect."

Mick tensed, and I put my hand on his arm. "It's okay. We were just talking."

"She's right. We *were*. But now we're done." Cooper threw his hands up, like he wanted to wash them of me, and then he backed away.

And I had a feeling that when he'd said we were done, he was talking about more than just our heated conversation.

Chapter Thirty-Three

I kept telling myself to stop obsessing over Cooper's and my heated exchange, and to definitely stop caring that I hadn't talked to him in days. After all, he'd broken my trust, one of the things I considered most important in a friendship.

Apparently we weren't friends anymore, either, and that realization sent a sharp twinge through my chest.

There was only one way to turn this whole situation around, and I figured at this point, I had nothing to lose. At lunch on Friday, I walked over to Mick and his friends, and when he glanced at me, I shot him the best smile I could muster. "Can I talk to you? Alone?"

"Sure." He told his friends he'd catch them later. As we walked out of the cafeteria, he put his arm around my waist and tucked his hand in my back pocket.

I hated that all I could think of was when Cooper had done the same thing—as a knee-jerk reaction—and then overwhelming longing rose up, and it was for the wrong guy, and why didn't my brain get it?

"That's not an option," I muttered.

"What?" Mick asked.

"Um, nothing." I swallowed and turned to face him, glad that it made it too difficult for him to keep his hand in my pocket. I'd thought when the time came, this would be easier. Clearly I'd thought a lot of things that'd turned out to be false.

My nerves frayed, and I convinced myself that was a good sign. It meant I cared enough to get anxiety over asking Mick the question I needed to. Unfortunately that thought didn't calm me nearly enough, because heaven forbid this be easy.

It's now or never. We're at T-minus three weeks and one day till prom…

Think about Dad. How he'd be proud that I did whatever it took to complete my Operation, despite all the bumps along the way.

"I was wondering…" My voice squeaked and I cleared my throat. "Jeez, I'm more nervous than if I were facing down a Lanister."

Mick's forehead scrunched up. "What?"

Oops. That only made sense if he watched *Game of Thrones*. Or maybe it didn't, because Cooper rarely got my references.

He did say my fandom tendencies were one of the things he liked most about me, though.

Another round of stabbing pain jabbed at my chest, because my thoughts were totally against me.

"What I'm trying to ask is…" I twisted a strand of hair around my finger, finding a tiny bit of comfort in giving my hand something to do. "Well, you know how prom is in three weeks…?"

"Yeah. It's all the girls at this school talk about—Paris goes on and on about how they need guys to help do the actual decorating, and under duress, I finally wrote my name on her damn signup form."

On the bright side, at least you're not making this one hundred times harder or anything. Since sarcasm wasn't doing me any favors right now, I shoved it away. "Will you go to prom with me?"

Mick took my hand and I waited for him to let me down easy. "Yes. I'll go to prom with you."

I blinked at him, probably way too many times and for absolutely way too many seconds. "I was almost sure you'd already have a date."

"A few girls have asked, but I was hoping to go with you. I even told my friends I was planning on it. I just didn't know if asking would seem too serious—didn't want to scare you off."

Aw, he actually thought about it. That's so nice. "Not too serious. I think it'll be fun, and you're the person I want to share my senior prom with."

And if I could go back in time to before I accidentally fell for Cooper Callihan, that wouldn't be a big, fat lie.

Chapter Thirty-Four

COOPER

Jaden got the green light to train as long as he kept his wrist wrapped, so he was healed and back to having full-use of his right arm again. We'd been putting in a lot of hours on the lake this week getting back to where we used to be. Which was good, since the Spring Festival race was on Saturday, just two days away.

If only I could gather enough strength to care.

My times with Kate weren't quite as fast, but the minutes between were so much more than rowing. A couple of ducks swam away from the boat as we neared, and I stared at them, thinking of the time Kate threatened to jump overboard to hang out with birds instead of me.

Jaden looked at the stopwatch. "The time's good, but you're off, man. This wouldn't have anything to do with Kate, would it?"

I jerked my gaze from the ducks and gripped my oars until the handles dug into my palms. "Nope."

"Liar."

I glared at him and he held up his hands. "I wouldn't say anything, but I saw Kate this afternoon, and she doesn't look so good, either."

"Funny. Every time I see her, Pecker's all over her." Toxic bursts of heat traveled through my veins.

"Maybe," Jaden said. "But her eyes go to you."

"Oh, so now you're an expert at girls?"

"Dude, I've *always* been an expert at girls."

I rolled my eyes, but I laughed. Probably the only time I'd laughed all week, too. Things just weren't as funny without Kate around. I tried to keep up appearances, going through the same motions I had before she crashed into my life and left her mark.

Everything pretty much went on the same as it had pre–Operation Prom Date, with the exception that Amber had started sitting with us at lunch. A rift had formed between her and Paris's crew. She'd gone on and on about it, and how she was *so over it*, so this time she wasn't going to apologize and try to fix it. Or something like that. Jaden and Alana had paid more attention to her occasional teary rants, because my head hadn't been right since I kissed Kate.

Our fight only messed me up more, and then there was the tension at home. Dad worked late every night, and the few times we shared the same space, an unspoken heaviness hung in the air. I kept expecting him to push the subject of my major, or to bring up more arguments in favor of becoming a lawyer, but he didn't bring it up. Almost as if the decision had already been made and written in stone, so there was no point in discussing it further.

Something I desperately wanted to talk to Kate about. I could really use her cheery optimism right now. I maneuvered the boat so it pointed back to shore, but Jaden dragged his oars. Since he seemed to be expecting me to open up and have a big share-fest, I gave him the shortest answer I could get away with. "She made her choice."

"Did you even let her know she had one?"

That brought me up short.

But what good would it have done? Why pour out my heart when I already knew she'd choose Pecker? If I had to hear her say that she'd rather go with him, it'd destroy the act I put on in the school halls, where I pretended to be okay. Why make a fool of myself and add to the suckfest that losing her in every possible way had brought on?

"You're really going to go to prom with Amber and just pretend everything's cool?" Jaden pressed on, because he clearly didn't know when to stop.

I dug down deep, pushing the oars through the water as hard as I could, since apparently I was rowing solo the rest of the trip to shore. The burn felt good in a way; it distracted from the other parts of me that felt broken. "I told her we could go, but we'd just be going as friends."

"How magical for her," Jaden said.

"You wanna go with her, be my guest."

"Careful what you say. I tend to take people at their word."

I dropped the oars and turned to face him. "You like Amber?"

He shrugged. Then he ran a hand over his hair. "I like Amber."

"You liked Kate, too, before I told you not to bother," I pointed out.

"Wrong. I said Kate was cute, and you looked like you might rip my head off for it, so I knew something was going on between you. But I like Amber. She and I have been talking a lot during lunch while you stare at Kate and pretend you're not staring at her."

I wanted to deny it, but I figured at this point, it didn't

matter. "If you like Amber, and she wants to go with you, I won't stand in your way. It'd be a relief actually."

"I'll ask." Jaden leaned forward, forearms braced on his knees, making it clear he was about to go all intervention on me. "But you need to talk to your girl."

"She's not mine."

"And whose fault is that? And don't you dare say Pecker's. Until you make a move, it's yours. You have to decide if you can live with that."

• • •

For the rest of the day, I couldn't get Jaden's words out of my head. I couldn't help thinking it was too late to do anything now, but if I waited and Kate and I didn't fix things before we graduated, I'd definitely lose her for good.

For some reason, that brought back one clear detail of Amber's ranting—somewhere in the mix, she said she'd regretted how things had ended with Kate, because she was an awesome friend, but she didn't realize how awesome until she was gone.

Mom walked into the kitchen, bringing me back to the present and making me realize water was spilling over the top of my glass, onto the floor. I quickly righted it and sipped at the top while kicking at the puddle to dissolve it—hopefully before Mom noticed.

"Why haven't you brought Kate over again?" Mom asked as she reached for an apple in the fruit bowl. "I didn't embarrass you that badly, did I?"

"Kate and I aren't really..." I let the rest of the sentence drop. Not hanging out with her anymore was hard enough without having to say it.

"That's too bad. I liked her. It does explain why you've been as testy as your father lately."

"Low blow," I said.

Mom flashed me her no-nonsense look. "I thought it might be more inspirational."

Great. Evidently everyone in my life thought I should be with Kate.

If only they could convince her, then we could all be happy.

She'll be at the race, I bet.

My mind started spinning on what I could say to her. On how to undo the crappy stuff and get back to the good—even if friends were all we could ever be.

I thought of when she'd first explained shipping people to me, and an idea started taking shape.

I just couldn't decide if it was totally genius, or totally insane.

Chapter Thirty-Five

KATE

I debated skipping the race part of the festival and sticking to the tented booths with crafts, handmade jewelry, and artery-clogging food. The occasional glimpses of Cooper that I caught during school made it clear that seeing him inflicted pain, even if from afar.

But all the hours I'd spent rowing made it hard to stay away. Not to mention the booths lined right up with where the race started.

I eyed the boats, alternatively hoping I'd spot Cooper's blond waves in the crowd, while hoping I wouldn't because of that whole aching thing.

"Looking for Cooper?" Mom whispered in my ear, and I jumped, nearly dropping my cotton candy.

"No," I said.

"Oh, right. The football player—that's who you like these days. I keep forgetting."

I fought the urge to stick my tongue out at her. Instead

I went for maturity and held the cotton candy out of reach when she tried to swipe a chunk.

Speaking of the football player, he was also competing, so I'd feel like a bad prom date if I didn't support him. Even if I had given up thinking we'd be anything close to exclusive—in the words of Tswift—*like, ever.*

But at least he no longer thought of me as a hookup girl. After he agreed to be my prom date, I explained that if he was going with me because he thought I'd be so grateful and caught up in dance-night magic that we'd hookup afterward, he'd be greatly disappointed.

He told me that as long as he didn't have to stop hooking up with other girls, he didn't care. Talk about romance, FTW!

Honestly, it was nice not to pretend to be someone other than who I was. The pictures would be stunning, and I could always point at the framed photo sitting among my Funko Pop figurines on my bookshelf and brag about how I'd gone to prom with the quarterback and possible prom king, which he was a total shoo-in for.

The only thing better would be going with the guy I could now say for sure that I'd loved, even if only for a little while.

Okay, considering I'd switched my cyber-stalking habits from Mick to Cooper—who didn't put nearly enough information online, FYI—I was possibly still in love with him. But considering his indifference toward me, I was trying to fall out of it.

Oh, look, there he is. The unyielding butterflies kicked up in my tummy, fluttering in that way they did just for him. He had his game face on as he picked up his number from the registration table. *Dang, he looks cute. And ripped and tall... Why does he always have to look so freaking hot?*

His waves were a bit wild, like he'd raked his hand through his hair several times. *He must be nervous.*

My fingers ached to reach out and squeeze his hand and

provide the comfort that I used to be able to. Unfortunately, it would probably only make him mad, and I didn't have stretchy fire-hose length arms anyway. Well, that last part wasn't unfortunate, but I digress.

Yep, looking at him now, my act of not caring about him, or how we weren't friends anymore, definitely digressed.

"You okay, hon?" Mom asked.

"I'm fine. I'm going to go find a closer seat to watch."

Mom glanced back toward the tents.

"Go get that necklace," I said. "And while you're getting it, ask for the farmer dude's number."

Mom's cheeks turned pink. "I don't know what you're talking about."

"Um, hello, the sparks were flying between you and the guy in the booth next to the jewelry stand. I saw the flirty smiles, too." I wrapped her in a side hug. "No one will ever replace Dad, but it's okay to date and move on, Mom."

In some ways, I needed to follow my own advice and not constantly be afraid that everything bad or hard that happened would only remind me of how much I missed him. I could miss him. I just couldn't let it hold me back from taking risks.

"I'm about to go to college," I continued, "and I know that I'm still going to live with you and all, but you don't want to be the sad woman who watches TV with a bearded dragon every weekend while I'm out at those raging college parties."

"Ha-ha."

"I'm serious; Klaus and I talked about it, and we both worry. He's mostly worried you'll get three cats, and he's not great at sharing the attention."

A smile broke free and Mom glanced back at the row of tents again. "He was really cute. And he did seem interested."

"Interested? There was shameless ogling on both sides." I shoved her toward the tents. "Now go. And don't come back until you've got his number."

Her laugh trailed after her, and I watched her go, a mix of emotions swirling through me, but the top one was happiness for her. Mom's willingness to put herself out there again encouraged me to stop being a wimp and head over to the stands. It might hurt to see Cooper, but I wouldn't let that stop me from enjoying the race. Or doing a little cheering for my former training partner, no matter what'd happened between us.

I spotted Mrs. Callihan in the crowd, and when she looked my way, I waved.

The guy next to her had to be Cooper's dad. He had the same blond coloring, but his features were on the austere side of the spectrum.

The thought of Cooper's expression eventually turning so serious, just to make his dad happy dug at me, and my feet propelled me forward. Luckily I was no stranger to making a fool of myself—might as well do so for a good cause, even if it ended up being in vain.

"Mrs. Callihan." I gave her a nod and turned to address her husband, my rapid pulse hammering behind my temples. "Sir, I know you don't know me, but I just have to say that Cooper's crazy smart, and he puts his heart into what he loves. I take full responsibility for him telling you that he doesn't want to be a lawyer, but I hope someday you'll realize that it'd be a shame if a career that made him unhappy drained him of his passion."

The lines in Mr. Callihan's forehead creased more with every sentence. With my piece delivered, my courage faded and the urge to flee took its place. "So…that's all I have to say. And, um, it was nice to meet you." I glanced at Mrs. Callihan, who beamed at me. "I'll be cheering for Cooper. Okay, bye."

"You must be Kate," Mr. Callihan said as I backpedaled— and in typical fashion—bumped into a passerby.

"Did I forget that part? Yeah, I'm Kate." I tentatively lifted my hand. "I'm a little afraid to shake your hand. Please don't crush it."

A low chuckle emanated from him. "Well, Kate. I know you don't think my son should be a lawyer, but I'm starting to think you'd make a good one. I think you might just stun everyone into agreeing with you."

"Thanks?"

"It's a compliment coming from him," Mrs. Callihan said, placing her hand on his arm. "A high one. And Cooper and his father are working on a compromise."

"We are?" Mr. Callihan asked.

"You are," she assured him in a tone I wouldn't dare disagree with.

"Really? I'm so glad." I bit my lip. "So yay and I'm sorry and I'll get out of your hair."

When I turned around, I nearly smacked into Jaden. "There you are," he said. "I've been looking for you everywhere."

"You have?" I lowered my eyebrows. "Why?"

"You can still row, right?"

"I haven't been training the past week or so, but I didn't, like, forget."

"Good." Jaden clamped on to my hand and started dragging me toward the row of boats. "I need you to be my partner in the race."

I dug in my heels. "No way. I came to watch the race, not to be in it. And even that's going to be hard enough for me."

Jaden spun to face me. "Cooper went crazy this morning and he says he's going to row with someone else because I'm not fast enough."

"Oh, Jaden, I'm so sorry." I patted his arm, trying to show him I understood but also that he shouldn't take it personally. "He just gets like that sometimes."

"You don't have to tell me twice about how he gets." He tilted his head toward the line of boats in the water, where people busily fiddled around with them, wiggling oars and stretching for their big race. "Just come be my partner. Please."

"I…" I had a feeling going out on the water to do something Cooper and I had done so many times would only add to the constant ache in my chest, but I didn't want to leave Jaden hanging—he'd been so nice to me. The added *please* made it impossible to say no, too, dang it. "Okay. But is Cooper all right? I talked to his dad and—"

Jaden's eyes widened. "You talked to his dad? That guy is scary."

I nodded. "Oh, for sure. But he's not as unreasonable as I thought." Which might be attributed more to his wife, but still. "Seriously, Jaden, I need to know about Cooper. Is he okay?"

"Depends on the outcome of this race," he said, his voice taking on a weird, cryptic tone.

Mick glanced up as we passed him and Vance, and he winked at me. "Wish me luck."

"Good luck," I automatically said. "Now that I'm in the race, you're probably going to need it."

The shock on his face made me laugh, but I couldn't dwell on it, because Jaden dragged me toward his boat at a breakneck pace, no stopping to smell the roses.

As my crappy luck would have it, Cooper's boat floated next to his, and Amber sat in there with him, in the front position. *He's rowing with Amber?* My heart cracked, and I stumbled as Jaden urged me into the boat. I didn't understand. Not how he could pick her over Jaden, and not why he wouldn't be taking the lead. She couldn't be strong enough to do it, could she?

"Take the forward seat," Jaden said.

"Have you done this before? Because that's not a good idea. I'm not a strong enough rower for that." *Just like Amber's not freaking strong enough.*

"Just trust me. I've got a plan."

What the hell was happening? "Everyone must've taken crazy pills today, or maybe I did, because nothing's making sense."

The mayor lifted a bullhorn, outlined the rules, and before I knew it, he shouted, "On your marks…"

"Just focus on the finish line," Jaden said as that crackling anticipation hung in the air, everyone ready to bolt the second the signal sounded out. "Don't look back."

I gripped the handles of the oars, figuring I'd give it my all, even if it was a useless cause. When the starting gun fired, I flinched, then dug my oars into the water.

The boat wobbled as Jaden shoved us off, and I resisted the urge to look back at him. That'd waste seconds and suddenly I thought maybe we would win. Who said we couldn't?

The push from the oars behind me shot us forward, one stroke after another, the movement so strong I dared a glance over my shoulder.

And dropped my grip on the oars. Instead of Jaden being there, Cooper sat there instead, rowing harder than I'd ever seen him go before.

"What the what?"

He dug the oars into the water again, pushing us farther across the lake. I glanced to the right, where he'd been in a boat with Amber earlier, to find Jaden seated behind her. I blinked, tried to remember if I'd hit my head at any point during the past few days, and then returned my attention to my swapped-out partner.

"Cooper. Hello? What's going on?"

"Just…a minute…and I'll…" He continued to row, the exertion making every one of those sexy muscles in his arms and chest pop. "Explain."

Since I didn't know what else to do, I grabbed the oars

and helped propel us forward. We were close to the lead, too.

But suddenly we slowed. I dug in my oars, but our progress wasn't nearly as impressive as it'd been a minute ago. One more row and I could tell my partner wasn't doing his part.

I glanced behind me. Cooper had abandoned his post and moved to the middle of the boat, his oars just sitting behind him, dragging in the water, which was going to totally kill our time.

"Whoa, dude, what are you doing? We're falling behind— you need to get back to your seat."

"I don't care."

"Yes you do. I've been in the boat with you before, remember? You've been training for this race for weeks, and we can still win." I grunted as I rowed as hard as I could, the boat gliding through the water, but not nearly as well or as quickly as before my partner completely lost his mind. "You just need to help."

"I need to talk to you."

"Okay, we'll talk after we win the race." I made another attempt to shoot us forward, but we were falling more behind by the second.

The boat wobbled as Cooper moved back into place, and I let out a sigh of relief.

I waited for us to start making forward motion again so we could hurry up and make up for lost ground. Instead the boat continued to wobble, and then Cooper's chest bumped into my shoulder as he reached forward and undid the fasteners holding my oars in place.

Then he just let them drop into the water. "Are you crazy?" I noticed his oars floating away from us as well.

"Yes," he said, and he placed his hand on my arm.

"We're going to lose the race." I motioned toward the other boats, now inching ahead of us—most a lot more than inches, actually.

"Yes," he repeated. "But I'm hoping I'll still win."

I ran my fingers through my hair and rested my palm on my forehead. "I think this must be a dream. The weirdest things are happening, and I don't understand it, and I'm just going to pinch myself and wake up, because this is going to be bad for my recovery."

"Your recovery?"

I shook my head. "In case this isn't a dream, I'm not making a fool of myself."

Cooper straddled the seat, one knee behind me, and one pressing against the outside of my knee. "It's not a dream. Because otherwise my heart wouldn't be pounding like it's about to bust out of my chest. I've never been so nervous in my life." He grabbed my hand and moved it over his heart, and sure enough, I could feel the steady beat.

This close, I could smell his familiar cologne. Could see the brown and green swirling through his eyes—eyes I'd missed so badly that I wanted to cry at the sight of them. And those dimples…close enough to touch. To kiss…

"Everything got all messed up, Kate. And I take full responsibility, because I broke protocol."

"Protocol?"

"On our mission. The deeper in I got, the harder I fell, and then I kissed you, and…" His gaze dropped to my lips and a shock of heat trembled through my core. "I can say with a certainty that you don't suck at kissing—that was the best kiss I've ever had."

Hope and happiness tingled across my skin. "Really?"

"Really."

"It was pretty amazing."

He nodded and leaned closer.

"Wait," I said. "You ruined your shot at winning the race to tell me that I know how to kiss? I just need you to be as clear as possible, before I start getting the wrong idea and end up with a broken heart. Because like I accidentally mentioned earlier, my recovery from you hasn't been going so well."

Cooper brushed his lips against mine and my stomach drifted up and up and up. "How's this for clear? I ship us, Kate. I want us to be Kaper or Coopte or Capote or whatever weird combination our names can make. You said something about forcing two people who were meant to be into a ship — obviously I took that very literally. You and me are my OTP, and if you don't believe me, I'm going to spend the next several weeks trying to prove it, until you ship us as much as I do."

A sound between a laugh and an ecstatic cry escaped my mouth. Then I crushed my lips to his.

Somewhere in the distance, I heard shouting in the bullhorn, something about a winner — possibly the announcement of one? — and how the boat that stopped halfway through needed to get out of the middle of the lake. But none of that mattered.

I threw my arms around Cooper's neck, parted my lips, and deepened the kiss, not caring that the whole town was watching, because I wanted them all to know that Cooper Callihan was mine.

As soon as I came up for a breath, I whispered, "I totally ship us, too." With that I'd had plenty of oxygen, so I dove right back in and kissed him again.

And again.

And again.

Chapter Thirty-Six

COOPER

"Well, Operation Prom Date is this close to being a success," I said as we stepped in front of the arched entrance to the dance. "Even if we ended up making a few modifications."

"Speaking of…" Kate ran her hand down the front of my white, button-down shirt. "I really like how your tux modification shows off your tall, ripped body." Earlier I'd complained about wearing the penguin suit, but if it meant she'd smile at me like that and run her hand down my chest, I'd wear the thing every damn day.

"If you think I look ripped in it, you should see me out of it." I waggled my eyebrows extra big and nudged her with my elbow. "Where was that on the Kanye Douchebag Scale?"

"I wanna say a nine, but since I saw you shirtless yesterday at the lake and know that you can back up the statement—not to mention you're literally listed in my phone as 'Tall Ripped Prom Date'—I'll go with a six."

I curled her to me and kissed the shimmery lips that'd

held me captive countless times over the past few months. "You are the sexiest, sweetest, best girlfriend ever. Did I tell you how amazing you look?"

"You mentioned it a few times."

When I picked her up and saw her in the dress, I was under the same spell that came over me the first time I saw her in it, back when I wanted to kick Mick's ass because he'd get to be the one holding her while she wore it.

Now here I was, running my hands over the silky ribbon at her waist and fighting the poofy skirt to pull her closer. Losing the Spring Festival race two weekends ago was the best thing that ever happened to me. Mick could have that win, because that day I'd won something way more important. "Well, it's worth mentioning again. You look absolutely beautiful."

Loose curls spilled down around her shoulders, and the braid at the crown of her head had sparkly stuff woven through it, giving her a Greek goddess look. She was like my very own constellation, one that guided me through the unknown.

She turned as Jaden and Amber approached. We rode over in a limo together, because I wanted Kate to have the perfect prom experience, and I owed both Jaden and Amber big time. It helped that my dad had a big soft spot for Kate, which meant he happily shelled out the money for it.

He and I were working on our relationship and had a deal in place. I'd complete a part-time internship with his firm this summer, and when I went to college, I could explore other options. As long as I was taking classes full-time and tried out at least one political science and one government class, he'd help me financially, regardless of what major I chose.

"You guys ready?" Jaden asked, wrapping his arm around Amber.

"Ready." Kate grabbed my hand and laced her fingers with mine.

We stepped through the star-shaped archway, into the decorated ballroom. Since Kate talked me into helping decorate, I knew way too much about what decorations had been used, and how they'd been hung. "After all," she'd prodded, "you know more about stars than anyone on the committee."

The things the girl talked me into.

I dodged a few low hanging stars and guided us to the open area near the edge of the dance floor. Dozens of couples filled the space, dancing under the twinkling lights. Others lined up to have their picture taken in front of the glittery shooting star. Over the top, a banner read "Wish Upon a Star."

For the past few months I'd wanted the ability to freeze time so I could enjoy every moment possible on the water. I'd never expected to want to slow down time at a school dance, but the pure joy filling Kate's features made me want just that.

I lifted our entwined hands and kissed the top of hers.

She snuggled in close, and I wanted to hold her and inhale her perfume and just savor every minute with this girl.

Luckily we weren't running on limited time. We had an entire summer of afternoons on the lake, nights under the stars, and endless kisses stretched in front of us. Then, in the fall, I'd go to Harvard, and she'd attend college in Manchester. The hour drive that would separate us was longer than I preferred, but when it came to being with Kate, it was nothing. We'd already talked about meeting halfway. I loved how she spoke about our future as if the only option was for us to be together, and for me, it was.

She was mine now, and I was never going to let go.

"Kate, hey!" Mick nodded at her and approached, leaving Paris to trail behind him. I wasn't a fan of how he addressed her but not me, as if I didn't exist.

When he hugged her and told her she looked beautiful, I became even less of a fan. I wrapped my arm around her waist and brought her flush to my side, barely resisting adding a growl. Kate flashed me a quick smile with a hint of *be nice* added. I supposed I should—after all, he'd agreed to let her out of their date so she could be here with me instead.

Still, I wouldn't be sending him a fruit basket soon or anything.

"Callihan." The acknowledgement was hesitant, as was my return nod.

"Hey, Paris," Amber said, and I think Paris tried to smile, but she didn't genuinely make the move enough for it to really work on her. Apparently she didn't mind being Pecker's backup option, but she didn't exactly look like she was doing cartwheels over it, either.

"You said we were going to dance." Paris tugged on Mick's sleeve and he sighed.

"Fine, let's dance." He rolled his eyes at me, like I'd get the hardship, and took Paris onto the floor.

Kate wrapped her arms around my waist and leaned in for a kiss. "Looks like I picked the right date."

"Looks like?"

She giggled. "Well, I haven't seen your dance moves yet."

"Oh, it's on." I grabbed her hand and pulled her onto the floor, anticipating spending all night with her pressed against me as we swayed to the beat. "Just remember you asked for it."

Chapter Thirty-Seven

KATE

Of all the times I'd imagined this moment, it'd never included a friend who'd helped me get ready—Amber and I started talking more after the Spring Festival race, and while we might not ever be the same, she'd apologized for the past and we'd renewed our friendship; a sense of accomplishment—I was at prom, feeling like a princess and wearing a dress I loved, and I swore I could feel my dad smiling down on me for pulling off my mission; and a boyfriend who I loved—even though I was still working up the courage to tell him.

In other words, tonight exceeded my wildest dreams.

Amber grinned at me as she and Jaden danced past us, and I returned her smile and snuggled closer to Cooper.

"And just so you never question my dance moves again…" He grabbed my hand, twirled me away fast enough that my skirt flared, and then spun me back into his embrace.

I laughed and put my hand on the side of his cheek, running my thumb down that delicious dimple. "*Now* I have no doubt I picked the right date. But I'll tell you a secret…" I tipped onto my toes. "There never actually was any question. You could be a horrible dancer and I'd still pick you."

"What if I stepped on your toes?"

"Who needs use of their toes? Totally overrated."

His grin widened. "What if my knee-jerk reaction is to…?" He slid his hand a couple inches lower on my back, and glanced around before moving it to cop a feel. Not that he could get much of one through the skirt.

Funny enough, that was when I felt offended, but more at the dress than the boy. "I'd be scandalized, but then I'd just teach you some better manners. Like it's really better to get both cheeks at once." I slid my hands around his waist and cupped his backside.

His wide-eyed expression made me burst out laughing.

Then we got a dirty look from the chaperones, so I moved my hands back to his chest and he moved his back up to the respectable range.

After the coast was clear and another couple was the target of the chaperones, I wound my arms around Cooper's neck and linked my fingertips. It brought our bodies close enough together that I could feel the rapid beating of his heart. Or maybe that was mine.

Our chests rose and fell together, and for a few magical minutes, every movement we made, we made as one.

The love I felt for this boy swelled, until every inch of me tingled with it. Once I'd thought that all boys were basically the same, but after spending time with Cooper, I knew that wasn't true. He was good and kind and smart and funny and he embraced my fandom side and told me that he shipped us. Was it any wonder I'd fallen in love with him?

As the song came to a close, I locked eyes with him. "I'm going to say something cheesy now… Just go with it."

The music transitioned to a faster beat, but Cooper kept

the slower pace.

"I don't need to wish upon a star," I said, "because this entire night is perfect, and being here with you is a wish come true."

Cooper drew me closer, kissed me, and rested his forehead against mine. "You should probably also know, Kate Hamilton, that I'm in love with you."

Euphoria surged through me, leaving every part of me pleasantly fuzzy. "I love you, too."

We kissed again, taking our time to do it right, with enough lips and tongues to gain the attention of the chaperones, as well as our classmates.

"So, I might not need any more shooting stars, but will you take me stargazing anyway?" I asked.

Cooper swept a curl out of my face and cupped my cheek. "Until you beg me to stop."

"Guess it'll be forever, then."

"I'm definitely okay with that."

And just like that, Operation Prom Date got classified as mission accomplished, and Operation Together Forever was a go.

Acknowledgments

This book was so much fun to write! Is it weird to thank your characters for being so fun to hang out with and easy to write? Well, I'm doing it anyway, because I'm weird like that. Working on this book also reminded me how much I love YA novels.

First off, I want to give a big shout out to all the fangirls out there. You're my people. May all the couples you ship find their way to each other. :)

I'd like to thank Stacy Abrams for all her hints about how she'd love for me to write a book for the Crush line, and then for making that book even better and shinier with all of her editing prowess once I'd written it. Big thanks to the Entangled Teen team. Alexa, Melissa, Crystal, and all the people involved in publicity, marketing, formatting, and cover design—I LOVE my pretty cover like whoa! I've worked with so many people on several lines at Entangled Publishing, and I'm always blown away by how amazing everyone is. I appreciate you all for giving me a home, and for the hard work you do to get my books into the hands of readers.

Gina Maxwell and Rebecca Yarros, on top of helping me brainstorm and plot, you girls keep me laughing and get credit for keeping me sane(ish). I'm so grateful to have such amazing friends! Rachel Harris, Melissa West, and Evangeline Denmark, thanks for taking the time to read a few chapters when I needed feedback ASAP, and for your friendship.

Big thanks to my daughter, Kylie, who is always happy to discuss ships and all things fandom related. You are a smart, strong, beautiful woman (I had to alter it slightly because not everyone gets *Bob's Burgers* references like we do-LOL). Also, thanks for all the help you do around the house so I can get more work done, and for being happy to hang out when I get some downtime.

To the rest of my awesome family, thanks for pitching in and for cheering me on, and for being kind and funny and for being understanding when I'm overwhelmed or fall short. Especially on cooking. One of you should really train to be a chef.

Last, but definitely not least, I want to thank all the readers. For reading and supporting me and for your kind messages that always come right when I need them. Because of you, I get to do my dream job.

About the Author

Cindi Madsen is a *USA Today* bestselling author of contemporary romance and young adult novels. She sits at her computer every chance she gets, plotting, revising, and falling in love with her characters. Sometimes it makes her a crazy person. Without it, she'd be even crazier. She has way too many shoes, but can always find a reason to buy a pretty new pair, especially if they're sparkly, colorful, or super tall. She loves music and dancing and wishes summer lasted all year long. She lives in Colorado (where summer is most definitely NOT all year long) with her husband and three children.

You can visit Cindi at: www.cindimadsen.com, where you can sign up for her newsletter to get all the up-to-date information on her books.

Follow her on Twitter @cindimadsen.

Discover more of Entangled Teen Crush's books...

ANY BOY BUT YOU
a *North Pole, Minnesota* novel by Julie Hammerle

Elena Chestnut's been chatting late every night with an anonymous boy. The boy can't be Oliver Prince, son of the family running the rival sporting goods store that's driving Elena's family out of business. The girl Oliver's fallen for online had better not be Elena Chestnut. She's the one girl he'd never even *think* of kissing. She's definitely not his online crush, because that girl is funny, sweet, and perfect. When Oliver asks to reveal their names at the Valentine's Day dance, their IRL relationship will either ruin everything, or they'll discover just how thin the line between love and hate really is.

THE BAD BOY BARGAIN
a novel by Kendra C. Highley

Baseball player Kyle Sawyer has many labels: bad boy, delinquent, ladies' man, fearless outfielder... Only one of them is actually true. But then sweet ballet dancer Faith Gladwell asks him to help wreck her reputation, and everything goes sideways. Faith needs someone to squelch the rumors she's an ice queen. And who better than the school's bad boy to show up her cheating ex? But her plan threatens to expose Sawyer's biggest secret of all...and that's a risk he's not willing to take.

WEDDINGS, CRUSHES, AND OTHER DRAMAS
a *Creative HeArts* novel by Emily McKay

Willa is happy to be the maid of honor in her dad's upcoming wedding. Not as happy about the best man being her soon-to-be stepbrother, the infuriating—and infuriatingly gorgeous—Finn McCain. Every time their paths cross, the attraction simmering between them grows a little harder to ignore. Willa knows Finn only wants what he can't have. But Finn is determined to prove to Willa that happily-ever-after will always be worth the risk.